# The Closet

## The Trials of Billy Wagner

### Book One

Ethan Falls

Fulton Books
Meadville, PA

Published by Fulton Books 2023

ISBN 979-8-88731-943-8 (paperback)
ISBN 979-8-88982-189-2 (hardcover)
ISBN 979-8-88731-944-5 (digital)

Printed in the United States of America

# CONTENTS

# CHAPTER 1

## A Child's Eye View

*It is in the dark that I cannot see, and it is in the
dark that my greatest fears lurk in silence.*

His name was Billy Wagner, and he was afraid of what was across the room in his closet. He had developed a fear of the dark, and it was the closet that his fear had become obsessed with. Now it was getting late, and his mother still had not gotten home from work. He was not sure what time it was, and he didn't know when she would be home to greet what remains of him. That was if what was in his closet had any inkling to munch on young boy bones.

He was sitting in his bed, and he couldn't move. For how long? Forever. At least, that was how it seemed as the minutes passed slowly. Part of the reason he couldn't move was the fear that had him so crippled that he thought the slightest movement from the closet would draw the thing from its hiding place and over to him in the dark.

The other reason that he couldn't move was that he had got to go to the bathroom. That was what had woken him up in the middle of the night, but he was too afraid to move to do anything about it. He was holding it, but for how much longer? He was not sure. The cramps had begun to get his legs shaking, threatening to reveal that he was here, that he was here waiting, waiting for the monster, waiting to be its supper.

He was lying here in bed, silent and watching for the slightest movement. He could feel his whole body locked in a tense struggle with his fear. The fear that was flowing through his veins, just as the blood pumping from his heart, made his skin tingle. Endless pinpricks touched his skin, from the tip of his nose to his legs as they shook. The fear was winning more by the second. Because of that, he was lying here, and the bathroom, out the door and down the hall, couldn't be any farther away.

It was getting harder and harder for him to stay in this bed, but running past a monster that was lying in wait to reach out and pull him into its secret lair and eat him alive kept him thinking that he would just stay right here: under his blankets.

The door to his closet was cracked open because he forgot to shut it before he fell asleep, and now it listened for him to rustle in his bed. It was waiting to see if he was awake or if he was asleep. If he was awake, it would crawl from its lair to snoop and sniff and devour him, if it would please, but only if it would hear him or if it would see him move. He heard that boys were a monster's first choice to eat. He guessed they tasted better. Or they just wanted to get rid of boys first. Which one was right? He was not all too sure.

His babysitter said that boys were like the devil and that they should all be beaten to rid them of their devilish ways. She said the devil was in a boy's soul. He didn't think that boys were her favorites. She seemed to hate them—boys, he meant. She was a nun for like a thousand years, but he was beginning to suspect she left being a nun to be an old lady out on Route 12 who devoured little boys.

He hadn't found the bodies of any dead boys yet at her house, but that didn't stop him from looking or wondering. She worked at a reform school for boys, so she probably had had a lot of boy troubles. *That sounds funny, I guess,* he thought to himself. *Boy troubles, she has probably had more trouble with boys than anyone in the history of the world,* he thought. She looked like she was as old as the world too. He giggled and then seized up, remembering the terror behind his closet door.

Being around boys all the time might make any nun crazy. He told his mom that his babysitter hated boys, but she didn't believe him. He told his mom all kinds of stuff, but she always thought he was making stuff up. Not that he hadn't done that, made stuff up. Didn't all boys do that when they knew they were trapped and had to find a way out of a tough spot?

If he made up a story, maybe his mom wouldn't know that it was him who spilled scrambled eggs all over the kitchen floor. "That's not lying," he told his mom. "Those are just other ways that it could have happened," he reminded her. She said it was lying, but storytelling and lying didn't mean the same thing. So he didn't lie to her, but he guessed she just wasn't the believing kind.

After school when he got home, his mom was at work. She didn't always work at night, but he read and played and waited for her to get home. He missed her when he didn't see her after school. After school, he came into his room, and he didn't mean to fall asleep when he did. But he just got tired, and he was "out for the money." He was not sure if that was what his mom meant when she said that, but it sounded good.

Usually, before he went to bed or before his mother put him to bed, he would make sure that there was a light on down the hall or that his night-light was on. His mom hadn't got him a bulb for his night-light yet, so it was up s———its for him now. "Maybe tomorrow," she said. Why was everything always tomorrow? "I'll get it tomorrow," she always said that.

He thought that was just parent speak for "I'll think about it." Think about it, that was another one good parent. He was beginning to suspect that there was a whole separate language that parents speak that kids just couldn't understand.

It was like some secret code. He meant he had secret codes and stuff like when he wrote in his secret Journal. He was hoping his mom didn't know about it, but if she did, he didn't think she could figure it out anyway. He knew his codes were good, but adult codes were just crazy confusing.

He didn't have a dad, but if he did, he couldn't even imagine having two parents telling you what to do all the time. Do this, do that. *Might as well just come right out and say it, Mom.* "You're in the shits, Billy." That didn't mean you had the real shits. That just meant you got real troubles, and waking up with no light on? That was real trouble, at least for him anyway.

Not having his mom in the house at night was scary at first, but he had started to get used to it. He told her he was just a kid and that he couldn't be left home alone. But after she started leaving him here by himself, he thought it was the greatest thing ever: to be by himself. She made sure he always had snacks, so as long as he could eat, he could stay alone. That was what he said to her, and they shook on it. He hadn't called her once at work.

The house creaked a lot at night when it was dark and quiet and when the traffic wasn't barreling down our road. The trees outside of the house were always kicking the house with falling timbers, sometimes startling him if they hit the side of the house hard enough. Sometimes it got loud, especially when it got windy out. Those were usually the nights that he got scared. The wind was blowing, and the rain outside sounded like raccoons trampling all over the roof.

Sometimes, he would hear noises and get scared, but he had a stack of blankets on the couch, so he would curl up into an invisible ball so no freaks or monsters could see him. "If you keep still, they will go away." That was what his mom said, and he believed her. But she also believed that if you ignore somebody, they would go away too. Maybe she thought people were like monsters in a way. He was still trying to figure that out.

He had been lying here, staring at the closet and letting it scare him even more every minute. He kept thinking about the sounds he was hearing and wondered if they came from inside his closet or somewhere else in the house. He lay still and kept quiet and listened hard. He was starting to get tired again, but there was no moving from this bed at all. He was too scared, and he needed to use the bathroom.

He wanted to make a run for the door, but if he went by the closet on his way to the door, he just knew that a big claw with long nails and skin melting off it would reach out and grab his wrist and cover it with a slimy melted skin slop when it clamps its hand on him.

He thought to himself that it was real, but how could it be? Nobody had ever seen a closet monster. You thought that there would be reports of monsters, but the cops never found any if they had to look. Maybe that was what dead bodies were when the cops found them. The bodies were the closet dwellers that had been caught unaware. Seen, they were dead on the spot. They might have been monsters, but when people saw them, they turned to a human form to hide their identity. If the one in his closet was seen by him, did that mean that it would die before it could sink its fangs into his neck? He guessed he was going to have to take his chances.

Goose bumps started to rise on the skin of his arms and the back of his neck as he was thinking about the monsters. Even curled up in the blankets on his bed wasn't keeping him from getting the chills. That was what all this monster-thinking had gotten him to. "Getting the bugs" was what his mom called it. "Goose bumps feel like little ants running down my arm, giving me the creeps," his mom said. That was what she said it felt like, and he thought about having a thousand ants crawling on his arms, and he thought he would rather have poison ivy itch all day long than menacing ants crawling all over him.

He was not home alone too much, but sometimes when he was alone and he got scared, that was when he wished he knew how to pray. But he didn't understand a lot of the grown-up stuff like praying. His mom would say "pray on it" on occasion, but he was not sure if she knew exactly how to do it either. After all, he'd never heard her pray. That was why he had never asked her to teach him what to say. She had said that he should just say whatever he wanted, but he was not sure if God would let him have everything he asked for.

Sometimes, he would ask God questions, but he didn't think he heard him. If he did, he wasn't saying a whole lot back, at least not now anyway. Maybe there was a long wait to get a response. Did prayer have to travel a long way? And what if the answer took just as long to get back? That could take forever!

Well, he didn't know a whole lot; after all, he was just a kid. He could read and write, and as long as he had books, he could usually keep himself pretty busy. He liked to write, and he loved to draw.

He asked his mom for a lot, but there were a lot of things that a kid, especially a boy, needed, like army men and matchbox cars and this and that. He didn't ever get what he wanted, but sometimes, his mom would throw him a dog bone and help a kid out.

He did make her mad though, and when she got mad, there could be some pretty colorful language going around, and she would throw out some colorful language without hesitation. He knew his fair share of good words, but she would get him a good one upside his head if she heard him use one.

After what seemed like forever and his legs hurt so bad that he didn't think that he could take it anymore, he heard a noise coming from the front of the house. He stayed still and quiet and listened for the noises that his mom usually made when she was coming home.

He heard the lock and heard her kick at the bottom of the door. Sometimes, it got stuck; and because the door was so heavy, you had to give it a good stiff whack with a foot.

He was so relieved that his mom was finally home. He took one quick stare at the closet door, and in one fast bolt-of-lightning-speed move, he threw off his blanket and jumped out of bed, ran past his closet door, and shot through his door to the bathroom. He slammed the bathroom door shut behind him but not on purpose. It went *wham!* when he closed it. When he sat down, he heard his mom calling him, but he had to poop so bad he couldn't even talk. It felt like his brain was going to blow out his ears.

# CHAPTER 2

## Mom and a Snack

His mom was putting away groceries and cleaning the kitchen when he went down the hall to the kitchen to see her. She looked really tired, and she looked like the tickle tummy bridge trolls attacked her with a weary stick.

"Hi, honey. Just so you know, it is late, and we have to get up early in the morning because I have to take you to Mrs. Ruth's. I picked up a few groceries, but I only had a few dollars, so we just have to get by for now."

His bad night just went from bad to almost impossibly worse. He could feel a pit in his stomach, and it replaced the appetite that he was just working into after seeing her with a new box of cereal. The first thing he thought of was digging his hand down in the cereal to get the prize. What kid could hardly wait to get down to the bottom of the box of cereal to get it? And his arm would smell like cereal all day. He would eat the whole box to get to it, but his mom would lose it on him for sure if he did.

Mrs. Ruth was his babysitter, and she was the ultimate torture queen. She had been watching him for the last couple of months, and he couldn't even think of anything worse than having to go to her house.

He'd rather be stuck in his room with the door closed, no light, and the closet door opened and just wait for the muse to come out and drip melting guts all over him as it devours his skull from the top down to his neck in small mangled chunks. Blood would splay the walls mixed with melted flesh that shook free from his face as it shredded away at his skull and tore off his face, then gnashed at his bones until it was so full that all it would think about was a nap. His mother would be saved by filling up the monster's stomach with his bones.

*I should be a skeleton for Halloween*, he said to himself.

He tried telling his mother that Mrs. Ruth was losing her mind and that she was crazy, but his mom thought she was just a lonely old woman who didn't have anybody to talk to. He knew she was about seventy years old, but that was all that he knew about her. His mom and Mrs. Ruth talked occasionally, but his mom didn't know anything about her either, other than she was a nun for a lot of years.

He wasn't exactly thinking when his mom finished talking, and without thinking, he blurted out, "I'm not going there!" It just snapped out of his trouble hole. Whenever he opened that hole to make sounds, sometimes he could get himself into a whole lot of trouble like he just did.

What he wasn't expecting was the flat-fingered hand that came in the exact direction of his left cheek. Then it made contact. The sting was amazing, immediate, and overpowering as it snapped him into a daze. He stood there motionless, and maybe he was waiting on something else to happen, but she didn't yell. *She sure let off on a good one that is for sure*, he thought to himself. He was glad that he went to the bathroom because he would have let go of all of it right then and there in his pants if he hadn't have gone already. That was all he could think of at that moment.

He stood there motionless as his mom had just stunned him to silence. "I'm sorry, Billy. I shouldn't have done that. I lost my temper, and I'm sorry." She reached out and ruffled his hair. He did still have bedhead from his stint in his room with the closet, so she wasn't messing up much.

She seemed like she meant it. He was waiting for more, but she stood silently, gazing at him. He was thinking that maybe she was busy in her head, packing a really big suitcase to take herself on a nice long guilt trip, but his mom wasn't like that.

She had tough skin, and she might feel bad at this moment, but she would go upside his head faster than a dog that was chasing a cat that was chasing a mouse that was pissed off that cheddar cheese was the name of a pig, and Mr. Mouse didn't stand a chance of getting any of that.

He stood there as his mom rubbed his head and his cheek and inspected the handprint that she just left imprinted on his cheek. Little did he know that that was just the start of a long twenty-four hours ahead for him. *Oh, let me have my bed and my closet at home. The closet you have is better than the one you can't get out of.* Anyway, because his feet still wouldn't work, he stood there motionless. "She slapped me so hard my feet wouldn't work," he pictured himself telling his friend this.

"She is crazy, Mom, and she is mean to me. She makes me do stuff, and I'm just a kid. I'm supposed to do fun stuff, not rake leaves and do dishes and clean her stupid house." Right then and there, he was about to lose it and start bawling his eyes out, but he held back. He didn't want his mom to see him as a weakling. He wanted to try and be like a man.

"You should be happy to be able to do something for someone else," she directed directly at him.

"But, Mom, she makes me do stuff. She's mean." He tried to get her to understand, but he could tell that she was starting to get angry, so he stomped over to the couch in front of the television and curled up in the blankets. He didn't dare speak a word.

"Don't turn that television on," she said to him. "I am going to bed. I have to get up early. I will get you up in time to get some breakfast. I love you. Good night." She sounded really mad, so he didn't even bother saying good night. Then he regretted it. He wanted to go into her room and hug her and maybe even curl up with her, but he was too mad and too tired to think of getting up.

# CHAPTER 3

## The Morning

Six o'clock the next morning came early. At least, it felt that way to him, and he could hear his mom in the kitchen, putting on a pot of coffee. She couldn't possibly start her day without one. At least, that was what she said anyway.

He told her good morning, and he was more than happy to inform her that he was completely and totally starving. "Could you please make me some breakfast, Mom?" he said from underneath his blankets before he could get moving. He was so hungry he just couldn't. Then last night came back to him in a flash. He heard them say that life goes fast across your forehead when you die just like bad feelings when something is creeping up on you. Last night, he felt guilty, and now he did all over again, asking his mom for breakfast. But he threw out a "pretty please" just to be safe.

"I'm making you some breakfast right now," his mom said to him as she ruffled through stuff, sounding like a freight train to his ears. She loved doing dishes in the morning, but that was what he got for sleeping on the couch. At least, that was what she said to him if he complain about all the noise in the morning.

"You need to get up and get dressed, and don't forget your blanket and a change of clothes just in case you need them," she said to him as she slammed a pan into a plate in the dish rack. He guessed she did it to get the blankets off his head, but he wouldn't guess to be right out loud and not to her this early in the morning—especially if she hadn't had her coffee yet. Sometimes, he tried to stay quiet so as to not bug her before her second cup, but his lips moved without him asking them to sometimes. Stuff just poured out between them and he couldn't help it. He just had a lot to say to her for being a kid.

Being a kid, you don't know a lot but "experience is everything." That was what his grandpa said anyway. He was old, so he had to believe him. He heard some old people know everything. The teachers in the ancient days knew everything, so his teacher at school knew everything too. That was what she told all them kids. But she wasn't old, so he thought she was either storytelling or lying, and he hadn't learned which yet.

"Thank you, Mom, for making me some breakfast," Billy said with a long look on his face as he stretched his arms and his back. His emotional roller coaster was about to crash-land on the planet everywhere: guilt for last night and not giving her a hug good night or the dread of spending the day with a babysitter who looked at you like a bear with a cub under each arm, just completely ready to eat your face off.

You never know when a parent is going to turn on you for not having expressed at least a little bit of gratitude. That was why he tried to tell his mom thank-you as much as he could remember to. He didn't think he ever remembered to, but most of the time, he couldn't remember if he could remember. Anyway, he thought parents needed to hear that just to keep them putting up with us kids. Parents are needy too, that's for sure. They will be the first to deny it, but they know that it's true.

"Hey, Mom?" Billy asked out as he threw off his blankets. The smell of French toast and scrambled eggs started to fill the air. Stomach pains began to sound off as his stomach swirled where it felt like a pit.

"Yes, Billy?" she replied.

"Why did the blind man stop skydiving?" Billy said as he got up and went and sat at the table.

"Why?" his mom said to him with a curious tone.

"Because his dog kept getting really scared," he said, watching his mother and waiting for a smile and a laugh, which came quickly.

She laughed genuinely as she set his plate down on the table in front of him and then ruffled his hair.

"I really need to go get ready for work," she said in a soft voice.

He knew that she was feeling bad for having to take him to Mrs. Ruth's. Deep down, he knew that she was listening to him when he told her things about Mrs. Ruth. He had never come home with bruises or any other injuries from her house, but that didn't mean there weren't any. *That old woman is mean and is losing her head*, he thought.

"I am working until at least six tonight, so I will pick you up as soon as I can. I'm not sure exactly what time I get off tonight, but I might have to stay late."

He felt his appetite completely drained down to his feet. That sickening feeling came back. It was such a bad feeling that it took him back to last night and the monster in his closet. It was just waiting for the right moment to come out and devour him, and it was that moment just before his mom got there that it was going to strike.

He knew he was there last night. He could feel its presence. He could see its face trying to peer around the edge of the door, trying to see him without being seen. Its teeth dripped with a drool that slowly flows down to the tip before it falls to the floor, bone lubricant. When it clamps its teeth down, the drool would ease the fangs into the flesh, his flesh, and if his mom was home, when it was done with him, it would come out of her closet next.

He looked at his plate, and what was once a breakfast fit for a superhero was now a pile of slop. He picked up his fork and, with no enthusiasm, began to eat his eggs.

"Can I stay home by myself?" he said as he dug at his French toast that he had been allowed to get cold because he was busy pouting and poking at his plate.

Brandy noticed that Billy's tone was sounding desperate more and more lately when she had to take him to the babysitter. She knew that he really dreaded going there, but what she could do about it right now was absolutely nothing. She knew that there was something that just didn't seem right with the woman whom she was entrusting with her son, but his overreaction was what was worrying her. If she overreacted and cost herself a sitter, then she would really have a problem. It seemed as if the problems had really been stacking up lately, and her chair was getting shorter and shorter, and the top was almost out of reach.

His mom grabbed him by the chin and lifted his drooping face up so that she could look at him. He did not want to look her in the eyes, but after a few moments, he looked up into her eyes.

After he looked up at her, she said to him in a soft voice, "I tell you what, this weekend, which is in two more days, I will take you to Toys "R" Us, and you can get one thing." As she said it, the light in Billy's eyes was there within an instant. She knew that she had hit the spot, and his demeanor shifted spontaneously.

"Really, Mom? Can I get a remote-controlled car? I always wanted one!" His excitement grew, and his breakfast became a thing of the past. He forgot all about it.

"If that's what you choose to get with your one thing, then I don't think that that is too unreasonable. Now finish your breakfast and get ready to go." For an instant, she thought that maybe she should say anything about going, but he didn't notice what she was saying after his head got thinking about toys.

She was relieved. Getting Billy out the door to Mrs. Ruth's house was a nightmare that she was not up to this morning. It was the desperate tone in his voice that had really gotten to her. She was sad this morning, and she didn't know why. She just felt sad. She wondered if her body was changing again for the umpteenth time in her life.

It was hard to stay positive when everything fought against her, but she knew that the two of them had come a long way. She knew they would be all right. The thought that they would be okay put a smile on her face.

"If I stay home by myself today, you won't have to buy me a toy, and I won't call you over and over again at work, I promise," Billy said in a last-ditch effort to change her mind about taking him.

"You know I can't leave you here all day by yourself. I wish I could, but I can't. A couple of hours are one thing, but all day is something else, so finish up your breakfast. We have to leave in thirty minutes."

*Oh my god*, he thought to himself as he began eating his cold French toast. He was so happy. One thing, he should never had said anything about a remote-controlled car. There were way better things to get than that especially if you were only getting one thing, and when his mom only said one thing, that was exactly what she meant. He hit himself up against the head with his fist for blurting out anything about a remote-controlled car. "*That was so stupid*," he said to himself.

Billy turned his head and watched his mother as she turned and began walking out of the room. He was happy she was his mom. He thought about all the times that he had given her a hard time in the mornings, and he began to feel bad about it. She was a good mom, and he knew it. He watched as she walked out of the room and down the hall to where, he bet, she lay in her bed at night and pictured and feared her monsters in the closet.

# CHAPTER 4

## The Early Years

"Harold?" she spoke with a soft, teasing voice, dragging the words out to slowly get his attention. "Ooh, Harold?" she said again. Her voice rose as she spoke his name, and her voice became more taunting than teasing.

He looked up at her and stopped what he was doing. She was beautiful, and she had all his attention focused on her at that moment, and she knew it instantly. She had him hooked with her voice.

At first, Harold wasn't certain that she was talking to him, but he was the only Harold there, and there was no doubt about that. He even entertained the thought, for a moment, to turn around and look behind him just to reassure himself that he was the only Harold present. He wasn't sure, so he waited. She looked at him with a determined stare. He stared back at her with an "I'm busy" look on his face.

As he looked at her with a mistrustful glare, she put her hand up and stuck up one finger and did the "come here" motion with it in slow motion, hoping to lure him. The smile on her face was the beacon, so she held it. He shook his head no. They gave each other a long look as both contemplated their next move. She put the prettiest smile on her face to say, "I'll be good."

He took a long look at her and didn't respond.

"Please?" she said softly to him. "Come here. I'll be good. I promise." She waved a hand, pleading with him. She stood there, looking at him, smiling as she waited for a response. Mere moments had become to seem like hours to her. This boy was almost not worth the effort. She would give him a minute more of her time, and then she was moving on.

Deep in her mind, she had begun to think to herself about the words she had just said and had forgotten all about Harold for a moment. "I'll be good." How many times had she said those words? "I'll be good" had become to mean something sinister to her. It had become to mean that she was no longer in control. But here and now, she did have control.

"Harold!" she said with a firmer tone. She figured maybe she should try something different. *Maybe*, she thought, *a threat or the sound of one would inch him closer.* If she raised the tone of her voice, she could intimidate him into doing what she wanted him to; and right now, she wanted the boy to come to her. *Maybe enticing him might be the only option*, she suddenly thought to herself as she was beginning to feel desperate. She waited a moment to see what he was going to do, but he just stood there, watching her.

"I'll let you pull my hair," she said softly, taunting him.

He looked at her as a smile started to rise on his face. With a little hesitation, he turned in her direction and faced her. His chubby cheeks bunched up, and the smile on his face became distorted. He had looked uglier and uglier to her every time she had seen him. She pitied this boy.

Harold stood there, staring at her for only a moment. He was looking into her eyes to gauge whether she was going to trick him. In a very slow motion, he took a small step forward toward her, and then, with a little hesitation, he took another. Slowly, he approached her, but he approached her as if she could strike at him with the hands that were hanging to her hips, bunching up her skirt with nervous hands. She waited painfully, hoping that he would not change his mind and turn around.

He was about two feet from the fence when he looked at her and said, "Really? I can pull your hair?" He knew she would never agree to such a thing, but a smile rose on her face. She had him, and she knew it.

"Yes, you can pull my hair. But first, I need one of your shoelaces."

"Why?" he said with a baffled look.

She saw the trepidation on his face as he squinted his eyes as suspicion began to crawl across it. She could see the coward in his eyes as she looked at him standing there, his fat belly bulging from underneath his shrunken T-shirt, and weren't all boys cowards? She had met plenty of boys, and she would have none as friends. *This boy's cowardice is of the worse kind though*, she thought to herself. His was that of a boy. Harold started to back up just a little bit. She sensed his hesitation, so she was quick to respond.

Rushing to get it out, she said, "The reason why I need one of your shoelaces is so I can put my hair up and tie it so you can pull it all, silly." She said it in a way that caused him to have such a big smile on his face that his fat cheeks gave him a second smile.

She sat down on the ground in front of him, her knees only inches from the square-linked metal fence that separated them. Now he was much taller than her, and he felt a little bit more at ease.

She pulled her skirt up above her knees as she sat there, waiting for him to make up his mind, slowly exposing some of her thighs. She was taunting him now, but he didn't notice what she was doing. She pulled her skirt up further on her leg, and she waited for him to look. She wanted him to look.

Harold looked down at her leg, and he saw that she was slowly pulling it up, exposing more and more of it. The nerves in his whole body began sending his limbs into almost a shocking frenzy. He suddenly became aware of all his senses.

"Okay," he said with a shaking voice as he stared down at her exposed skin. He got down onto one knee and began to untie his shoe as she watched. He stopped as he was pulling the lace and looked up at her. Her eyes were gleaming. They were impatient eyes. She was watching him. She was waiting for him. He began pulling the laces through the eyelets of his shoe again faster and faster, one side at a time.

His hands were shaking, and untying his laces was the only way to get them to stop. After he pulled all the lace out, he bunched it up into a ball. He reached his hand out to hand the lace to her through the chain-link fence, but he hesitated. "Do you want to see my fort? It took me two days to build it. You can come in, and we could decorate it," Harold said with his pride showing as to dissuade her from thinking that he was staring at her bare skin intently.

The four-foot metal chain-linked fence stretched the entire length of the property line that separated their two backyards. Harold liked to hang out back here because there was lots of fun stuff to do like build forts and tepees. Trees and saplings were plentiful, and you could get lost in some of the woods that covered the entirety of the western part of the large piece of property. Harold played up in the trees, and he kept himself busy but never too far out of the sight of her when she saw him back here, playing.

Hesitating, Henry reached his hand out and gave her the balled-up piece of shoelace through the square metal hole in the fence. She was careful not to let him touch her. He was dirty. Boys were dirty.

With a really big smile on her face, she said, "Put your hand through the fence, and I'll show you a special kind of knot that I know. It's really neat." She knew she would need to use a convincing demeanor to lure this irritating seven-year-old boy into her trap. "I saw it at a magic show last night." She looked at his large belly and struggled to keep a smile on her face. *He probably eats twelve sandwiches a day*, she thought. *That's not including snacks, and the snack is probably apple pie.*

He sat down in front of her, looking at her. He didn't move.

"It's okay. I'm just going to show you." She was so convincing.

"Okay," he said back to her with no hesitation in his voice.

The thought of learning something new had him hooked. He was the really smart kid whom his parents were always bragging about. It just made her sick to hear about him all the time. They said this kid was really smart. Well, she was going to show them just how wrong they all were.

He slowly stuck his hand through the fence, wiggling it to get it to fit through the hole in the fence. As soon as he did so, she grabbed his hand around his fingers so that he could not move them. She took the lace and wrapped it twice around his wrist and tied a knot.

"Did you see it?" she said, putting her hands up in the air like she accomplished a huge feat.

"See what?" he replied to her, totally confused. He was starting to get irritated with her and began pulling his hand back through the fence. She grabbed it and held it tight to keep him from pulling it back anymore.

"The knot I made!" she said it loudly, trying to make him feel dumb. "It was like magic. Didn't you see it?" She looked at him like he was making her feel bad. "Put your other hand through, and I'll show you again." She looked at him and expected him to turn around and run any moment, but to her surprise, he stuck his other hand through the fence.

She grabbed his hand when he stuck it through the hole, quickly as to not let it escape. She was moments away from having a prize. She couldn't let it get away now. She pictured his hand like a snake, trying to wiggle itself free in her hands. If it was in her hand, she would squeeze and squeeze it until she couldn't anymore.

This time, she held his hand really tight as she wrapped the lace around his wrist. She began to slowly squeeze his fingers as she wrapped the lace as tight as she could get it. Henry began to wince. The smile that was all enticing to him minutes ago was now replaced with what couldn't be misconstrued as a snarl. She made sure that it was tightly wound. Then she made a knot and pulled on it to make sure that it was really tight and that he wouldn't escape it. He winced and asked her to not be so rough as she finished tying his wrist.

"There!" she said, all proud of herself. She threw her arms up in epic triumph.

"I didn't see it. Show me again!" Harold said, his frustration growing quickly as he began to tug at the laces that had both wrists bound closely together, double wrapped to give the laces more strength. He was a big boy for his age, so she had to be sure.

With a real snotty tone in her voice, she said, "What do you mean show you again! I just showed it to you twice!" Her mocking tone put a look on his face that said "you tricked me." His eyes grew wide, and his lips began to squeeze at each other, locked in a struggle of pressure, one against the other.

He didn't think for a moment that she wouldn't show him again. After all, she said that she would show him. If he didn't see it, she had to show him again. That was the rule as far as he knew it. He wanted to see the knot, and she didn't show him. It wasn't fair. He started to get a frustrated look on his face after tugging on the fence a few more times, but this time, he started to pull really hard on the fence, almost bringing it to his chest in the tug-of-war, him against hundreds of feet of fence. It didn't seem fair. He was certainly stuck. That was for sure. "What was he going to do?" raced through his head.

"You didn't see it?" she kneeled closer to him and just stared at him. She waited and watched him as his mind was busy trying to figure a way out of this mess. She looked at him, slowly moving her face closer to the fence.

"That's because you're a stupid boy!" she snarled out at him. She got up to her feet and looked down at the boy. He got a look on his face that said "Uh-oh, I'm in a real big jam. I'm in such a jam I got peanut butter wanting me!"

She began to hum as she looked down at this pathetic boy. She shrugged her shoulders. She turned and began slowly walking down the fence line, ruffling the sides of her dress as she went. As Harold sat their struggling to free his hands and screaming for her to let him free, she slowly disappeared down the hill and out of view.

Down near the back corner of the property was where she liked to go. Down there, the trees lit up the sky with autumn colors that just painted the sky when you looked up into them. The bright oranges and golds captured her attention, and she couldn't look away from the colors. Leaves floated past her, guided by breezes jetting down the hill in her direction. The smell of the leaves separated from the tree host for the season filled the air with a distinct smell that could only be captured a few weeks of the year.

She felt at peace. The quiet encompassed her, and she was able to just let it all go, her stupid mother, her stupid father—all the people who wanted to tell her to do this and to do all that. Phooey on all of it, she just wanted a little bit of peace. She just wanted to look up into the sky and feel the warm sun on her face. She was content. Then she heard it.

Her moment of peace was invaded by an alien sound. It was faint at first, but then it slowly got louder and louder. She listened as the boy began to scream. She listened to the distant moans of disbelief. She began to smile.

She listened to the panic that had already begun to creep its way into the boy's head. In the next hour, it would be a complete panic. After that, it would be thirst, then hunger, and the afternoon sunshine. As she stood there, looking up into the beautiful golden leaves above her, she pictured in her head what his struggle would be like.

She turned around to make her way back to the house. She looked down and saw a stick about four inches thick. It was like a baseball bat. *She never had one of those*, she thought to herself. She picked up the large stick. She turned to a large, thick tree behind her. She looked at it for a minute as the cries in the distance rang out.

As hard as she could, she swung the large stick against the side of the tree. The vibration of the collision set off thousands of nerves in her hands, and the pain was energizing to her. She welcomed it like a new dress. She hit it again and again until finally the large stick snapped in half. She threw the half in her hand to the ground. She turned and began humming and walking back up to the house. *Lunch maybe?* she thought. *Perhaps.*

Drops of blood slowly made their way down to the tips of her fingers. There they gathered, and all at once, they fell to the ground, leaving a trail back to from where she came.

# CHAPTER 5

## Brandy

It had been a really stressful couple of months for Brandy Wagner, not that the last few years had been very much easier. As a matter of fact, now that she was thinking about it, there really hadn't been too much time through the course of her life when life was easy.

When she was with Billy's dad, those were about the best years of her life, but they were stressful years. Being a military spouse could sometimes come to a head especially when times of struggling financially added more stress than the war side of the equation did.

The worry for a spouse could be really taxing on some people. Some people worried just to worry, and that was probably the category of type of person that she would fit in. The worry gave her ulcers, and that, she would testify, was awful. They had a lot of really good times together. They had a couple of good arguments, but they made it through everything that was thrown at them.

It was their love for each other that got them through a lot of things, especially him being gone for long periods of time. Sometimes she got so depressed that she felt completely cut off from the whole world. She felt like she was literally trapped in her own body. It took her a long time to recover from the trauma.

She hated to think about all that happened back then and Billy and how it all affected him. Not having a father had been tough for him, and she knew that, but she was really hopeful that that could change sometime in the near future.

It took her a long time to even contemplate dating again. It was foreign to her, and frankly, once she settled in on a routine with Billy, she really didn't need anybody. She simply became content with the way that things were. Slowly, she had worked and eventually bought them the house. It took a lot, but the two of them had come a long way together and went through a lot together.

You would think that being a single parent and having only one child should not be that difficult to navigate. It was all the other stuff that really got the spokes flying off the wheel. She had been going through problems at work and navigating that mess plus raising Billy. It hadn't been easy. Then there were Billy's grandparents and everything that they were going through. Add on a new male acquaintance and there was overload.

Four months ago, she met Alex, and they began dating. It was a slow start, and the relationship truly wanted to fizzle even before it began. She did not think that it would work out between them frankly because their first date was so damn difficult to accomplish. Between both of their schedules, neither one had time at the same time to go out on a date.

Then they met for the first time, and the evening went horribly wrong for the both of them. A waitress spilled a cup of coffee all over Alex's back. It was a disaster in the middle of a really good meal. Being gracious to not make the situation even worse, they decided to leave.

The burn and the stain were quite good enough excuses for anyone to call it a night. Then, in the process of them leaving, Brandy hit a waitress and her tray, sending it and her sprawling. Neither one of them felt too confident in the rest of the evening. End of date.

Two weeks later, they had discovered that the two of them together really could enjoy each other's company. Hiding the relationship that blossomed out of nowhere from Billy had not been easy for her, and she never felt good about it.

She wanted to think that she was protecting Billy, but she knew that she couldn't protect him from everything all the time. As much as she tried, she had to force herself to let it go. What she didn't want to do was to tell Billy about the relationship, and then the relationship went sour three months later. She felt stuck in a catch-22. It would be a disaster for her and Billy if she told him and he got attached and lost it again. That was her greatest fear.

After a couple dates with Alex, after getting past their first-date disaster, he had swept her off her feet. He looked tough, but he was the kindest man that she thought that she had ever met. She had not been swept off her feet like that since her and Billy's dad had their first date, not that she wanted to even try to compare the two, but thinking back, she realized just how long it had been since she felt true love between two people. It had been almost a whole generation between loves for her. Alex became more than she could have hoped for though.

She had dated a couple of times in the last year, but she kept going back to the "nothing measures up" mentality, and the two relationships became nonrelationships really quick. She was worried at first that it would happen to her and Alex, but after spending a day with him, she felt so at ease, and yes, she even thought it could work.

Alex didn't have any children, but that was not by choice. He had always wanted them, but he was unfortunate enough to have found the right person. He had been asking her recently about meeting Billy, and that was when she had sprung it on him. She told Alex that she was pregnant, and he couldn't have been happier at that moment.

*It looks as if Billy will get to have a family after all*, she thought to herself after telling Alex the news. Tonight, after picking Billy up from Mrs. Ruth's house, her and Alex were going to share the news with Billy together over a nice dinner. It had been a long time since she had taken Billy out to a really nice place, and she hoped for the best and wished the day wouldn't drag on forever. She even felt a little bit of excitement.

Having to take Billy out into the middle-of-nowhere village to get him looked after by a devil sister didn't exactly sit too well with her though. She felt terrible. It was a lot easier with his grandparents around but that was another time. For now, she had to just get through today. For that matter, she just had to get through the week, and then the next month. It never ended.

# CHAPTER 6

## The Departure

Billy and his mom carried all their stuff out to the car. He had his arms full and was trying to keep his blanket from falling on the ground. A couple of times, he stepped on the corner of it and almost went face-first into the driveway. However, he was careful not to make his mom mad; she didn't always stay the cheeriest person in the morning. He was sure that he was the reason she got mad though. A lot of the time, he would get yelled at, but if he didn't do really stupid stuff, sometimes she would stop and get him a snack on our way out to the boonies or the middle of nowhere, as his mom liked to say.

They both got into the car and got their seatbelts on. His mom wouldn't move the car with him in it if he didn't have it on. "Windshield face is a hard way to go through life, Billy," she would say if he didn't buckle before she had to tell him.

His mom pulled out of the driveway and onto the road, but he curled up into his blanket. It didn't take but a couple blocks, and he was out like a light. The next thing he knew, he heard them pulling into the driveway off Route 12, where he was sure that Mrs. Ruth had the body of the dead boys whom she had babysat before him or any kids who had come trick-or-treating in the last decade or two.

The gravel driveway was long, and he could hear the tires slowly crunching away at the little rocks that led their way through the overgrown trees and bushes that lined their path. It made seeing from the road all but impossible. It was like a haunted mansion hidden from view. You knew that it was there, and you knew the windows were all broken out, but all you had was the picture in your mind. Here at this place, he got the real thing every time.

They crept their way up the driveway. Slowly, the dark shadow of the house began to come into view. It lurked menacingly in the distance at first, but then it came closer. It was like a vegetative wonderland. Trees, ivy, and bushes wrapped the house and insulated it from outside view. If the house was painted, it was painted black, maybe like the black heart of a darkened soul who inhabited it.

They pulled up by the house, and the silhouette of the house gave him the instant creeps. The clouds were dark, and the moon disappeared behind them, so the front of the house looked like it was silhouetted only by night. It always gave him the creeps coming here. He had always been scared here. He wished he could tell his mom, but he didn't think she would understand.

At the start of the summer, before he started to get dropped off here, he was having very scary nights every night. He kept seeing and hearing monsters at night, and she was always tired because of him. Some nights, she would let him come sleep in her bed. But the night—he saw and heard them in the night. The night was always the loudest. She said he imagined too much.

You don't hear the sounds of the night, not really. You are bombarded with the loud voices of the day like trains, cars, subways, buses, and horns and phones. But when night comes to you, it sounds like silence, peace, or quiet. But to him, the night was noisy.

He heard the creeks in the house and outside, and he knew they were there. He knew they were waiting for him. He knew that they were watching him. He could feel it. He could feel it in his bones. He could feel them and their presence.

His mother said they were not there, but he knew they were right around the corner. His teeth chattered when it got bad. His fear grabbed him, and it squeezed him so tight that he could hardly breathe, and when he did breathe, he gasped. Then it heard him. He had let them know that he was here and that he was prey for any or all. At any time, it could be him that they would devour in the night.

He couldn't help screaming at night. Now she didn't have patience for a lot of things that she might not see or believed. But he believed. He knew.

His mom stopped the car up close by the house in the same spot she always parked in. They got out of the car, and his mom helped him gather his things. His eyes were still half closed because he just felt so tired. He had to fight to open them. It was just so hard. He didn't want to stay awake for anything, not even if his mom were to hand him a dozen doughnuts or a cake. If he closed them at this very moment, he would fall asleep, standing up.

The leaves were blowing across the yard, and the wind added a cold to the air that sent chills up his back. He had a jacket on but without gloves or a hat; the wind ate at his skin with a nip that was felt from his head to the tips of his toes. Even his hair was cold. Well, that might not be true, but maybe he could feel it with his hair. It hurt like a holy one when it was pulled, so he guessed feeling hairs was true.

The leaves from the trees had begun to fall, but the brilliant colors of them were hidden by darkness. They blew across the yard and into the vegetation, holding out open arms so that all of them together could disappear into the winter's snow.

There were piles of them everywhere and along the front walk stones; they became barely visible as the leaves packed themselves at the edges. He dreaded the thought that she was going to make him pick all of them up. If he were out here for a year, he would still never be able to get them all.

# CHAPTER 7

## Anne-Kay Ruth

Anne-Kay Ruth, known years later as Sister Ruth, was born to an upper middle-class couple in a neighborhood outside of the city of Detroit. Her mother was a deeply religious person, although if her views had a positive effect on Anne, you wouldn't have known it. She tried to instill her religious beliefs into Anne as she grew up, but Anne was a strong-willed little girl, and there was no making Anne do anything that she wasn't willing to do.

Anne was born before her time was due, and it might have been that early entry into the world that made her younger years so diffi-cult. She was a beautiful baby girl, but she cried relentlessly as a baby. Her health problems might have played a big role in her nonstop crying and screaming. She was rarely content as a child, and her dis-comfort made the home a very tense environment. That was because nobody in the home could sleep past her restlessness.

Her mother and her father were living a life of duress with a child who never stopped crying. Perhaps that was why her father had taken a job where he was in another state to do his work. Even those who worked in the home for the Ruth's had little patience for the child who would, in the coming years, test the will of all who were working in the home. Many would find out the hard way that Anne would be the one who would make the rules in the home.

For the first five years of Anne's life, she was a very sick child. Illness after illness struck her, and Anne almost died during several severe bouts with pneumonia. Her immune system was very weak, and if there was an illness that could be had, she would be the first to get it. The doctor had come to the house on so many occasions when Anne was a child that he could have scheduled regular visits to the home.

Her mother sat by her bedside and wiped her forehead and cared for her during a lot of those illnesses. Her mother was probably the only reason that Anne survived her childhood, caring for her with the patience of a loving mother. Anne's mother was there for her when she was younger, but as Anne grew past the age of six, the memories of her mother began to fade. Anne did not remember the last time she saw her mother because even though she was a member of the household, she was rarely present.

She was extremely conflicted with her mother. She was torn between the woman who had sat by her bedside night after night and the woman who had come to turn her back on her at the turn of a screw.

Her father had become a politician, and because of that, he was rarely seen by either Anne or her mother during the coming few years. His distance kept him from being home more regularly than he should have been. His obsession became wanting what others wanted and taking what he was able to take.

Anne made it through her younger years, and her bad health became more than her mother could handle. By the time that Anne was seven, her ability to torment had been rooted, and her ruthlessness held no bounds. The people who came to work at the house had become targets of Anne, so the house became a very toxic environment.

Anne had begun to do things that had her mother living in fear. By the time Anne was thirteen, her mother was at her wit's end and tried to avoid Anne, her own daughter, all together. She had finally confronted her husband who was oblivious as to what had been happening in the home with his daughter due to his absenteeism.

It was fear that guided her mother through the last several years. One day, her mother made herself tea and sat in the sunroom, admiring a beautiful, warm, sunny Michigan afternoon. The summers could get really hot, but she didn't mind. The house was quiet, and she was able to sit and relax and get herself a quiet moment. As she gazed off at the back of the property, she noticed something just a little odd.

There was a little figure in the distance that did not seem to be there early this morning. Out of curiosity, she took her tea and began walking out to see what had captured her attention. When she got to the back fence line, she noticed a young child's lifeless body. It was Harold, Cathay and Dan's son. His hands had been tied through the back fence with his shoestrings. The young child had been exposed to the sun all day and was burned and almost lifeless. She did not need to know the details of what had happened. This was Anne's doing. She knew it.

Anne had come close to almost being responsible for the death of a neighbor's child. That was probably not her intent, but Anne's mother was not so sure. It was six months after that that her mother had had enough of the antics of Anne's. Her mean ways and her antics had been a test of her mother's patience.

# CHAPTER 8

## The Haunted House

It was almost Halloween, and this place in the dark was just about as scary as any place he had ever seen. If he ever wanted to go to a haunted house, this place was what he imagined a really good haunted house would look like.

The two cone-like structures at each end of the house made the middle of the house, where the front door was, looked like it was reaching out to pull you in and then drool while thinking of gnawing on your bones as it pulled you in.

The cold wind had him both wanting to run for the front door to get in, yet his feet felt like bricks because he did not want to go. It was so hard to walk up there to the front door. They made their way up the front walkway as the wind was seemingly hitting them from every direction.

The leaves made whirling circles in the dark, along the ground, and up high where the birds waited quietly and hunkered down until the winds were less remorseless to blow them off course. He dredged up the front stairs and followed his mother to the door.

She opened the heavy wooden front door without knocking. The house's inhabitant was agitated easily and knocking was a good way to start off a bad morning. There was a long squeal from the aged hinges that gave away our arrival. She knew we were here. It was at that moment that had a dog—or a wolf, perhaps—been present, the first howl would have rung out.

Slowly, they entered the foyer, and the cobwebs lapped in the corners from the breeze of us walking by. The air was still, and the temperature made it a welcoming environment for all things that liked to creep and crawl.

Some of the spiders here were bigger than he ever could have imagined that a spider could be. He had seen them. Just add fangs to any of them and make them bigger and humans might find their way lower down the food chain.

The spiders were not visible, but he knew they were there, watching. They were there hiding, and he could sense them peering down at him. He looked slowly up into the corners of the room to see if he could find them as he slowly walked forward behind his mother. He was both using her as a shield and at the same time trying to hide from view as closely behind her as he could get. He had finally begun to walk so close to her that their feet almost got tangled, sending both of them sprawling.

He loosened his grip on her after that and followed behind her the rest of the way, feeling distanced from her as the spiders stared down at them from every direction. The path to the living room, in the far back of the house where the heathen haters belched out their calls to repent echoed from the box that was to be watched throughout the day, was narrow and piled with stuff—junk, as his mom would say.

The house was the home to everything that one person could want over a lifetime and then a little more. The house was as if nothing had ever been thrown away. A lifetime of collected photographs clung to the walls as if they were permanently embedded there. Stacks of items made yet more stacks for more things everywhere you walked. Each room had its own collection of related room regalia.

The dust and the cobwebs competed for places to cling in all but those well-used areas where they were not apt to stay long. Cleaning either one regularly would only invite more. He couldn't imagine more than there already was.

His mom directed him over to the couch in the living room where he could lie down and sleep. It was old and worn, but it was comfortable to snuggle up on. His mom went into the kitchen where

Mrs. Ruth was likely getting doughnuts taken from piles of boxes of doughnuts in a cabinet next to a dozen boxes of Jiffy mix, her next favorite snack.

He couldn't hear what they were saying over a man yelling out on the television that God will "strike down the sinners and repent," as he kept saying. The nonstop quaking from people in two different directions made him want to slumber. *Why can't it all just stop so I can sleep?* he thought to himself. He pulled the covers over his head and drifted off as the quaking in the background continued.

"Goodbye, Billy," he remembered his mother saying as she planted a kiss on his forehead. Her lips were soft to the touch, and he could feel her love for him with just that little gentle touch. He had fallen asleep, but he had remembered that much. It would be the last time that he would ever hear her speak those words.

# CHAPTER 9

## Anne's Way

The sun was shining through Anne's window as she woke up and yawned and stretched her arms out as far as they would reach. The warm sun felt good on her face as she lay there, contemplating what it was she felt like doing today.

She knew that being out in the fresh air was what she most wanted to do. It would do her a world of good to not be stuck in the house all day. Yesterday, it rained all day, and by bedtime, she was getting cabin fever and feeling at odds with herself.

When she was done waking up and getting dressed for the day, Anne made her way downstairs to the dining room where breakfast was waiting for her.

Anne sat with her mother as she ate her breakfast, but two words were not exchanged between the two of them. Anne was not a pleasant person in the morning, and her mother knew that, so she just let Anne sit in her quiet world as she shoveled toast and fruit into her mouth.

After she finished eating all her breakfast, Anne rose from the table and told her mother that she was going to go for a walk and to play outside. Her mother was relieved that Anne would be out of her hair for a little while. With that, Anne was out the door.

Anne made her way down the front walkway and began walking down the street, looking at the large homes spaced far apart from one another. She walked past the Livingston house where the creek ran past on its way into town. She noticed that there was a boy play-ing down by the creek, and she was curious as to what he was doing.

With no interest in hurrying, Anne began walking in the direc-tion where the boy was squatting down by the riverbank, doing something. As she got closer, Anne watched the boy as he was build-ing a dam in the water. She was fascinated with what he was doing.

She watched him as she stood behind a large oak tree, out of view of him or anyone else passing by. For what seemed a while, she watched him; but as she did, she slowly began to creep herself closer to where he was on his knees, sizing up sticks.

Stealthily, she crept forward. She did not want to give herself away just yet. He was working diligently with the individual sticks, sizing them up for appropriate thickness required as she peered on in amazement at his patience. Now and again, he would go on a foolish quest for more sticks and rocks. Back and forth he went while she watched from twenty feet away.

She watched as he made mud slurry and crammed it in with the sticks as he weaved them together. As she got closer and closer, she tried harder and harder to not make a noise. Now and then, she would kneel so it was harder to see her if she made a noise.

He did not notice her approach behind him at all. He was so fixated on what he was doing he probably wouldn't have noticed a herd of deer walk by him. *He is crafty*, Anne thought to herself. She approached him closely and inspected his work as close as she could get without her feet getting dirty. The dam that the boy was making would have made any beaver jealous.

"What are you doing?" Anne said to the boy as she began try-ing to look over his shoulder. She intentionally tried to scare him by speaking loudly.

The boy was startled by her voice and spun around, stunned to see who it was. He looked at her, and his heart instantly stopped. Her beauty and grace had made him feel as though a princess had just walked up on him. For a moment, he forgot all about what he was doing and stood there, staring at her.

"What are you doing?" she said again softly. She was so pretty that it had him lost for words. He didn't know what to say. He had never seen her before, and he was taken by surprise at this beautiful girl who took an interest in what he was doing.

"I'm building a dam. Do you want to help?" the boy said to her. He grabbed some mud to show her, thinking that she would be impressed by it.

She was appalled to think that this boy would think that she would want to help him, especially with all the mud he had all over himself. The boy was a filthy mess. She looked down the front of the boy, and he had mud all over him.

She stood over him and looked down at him. If he would have looked up at that moment, he would have seen a look of disgust on her face. She stepped back, careful not to get dirt on her shoes.

"How about I just sit here and watch you?" she said to him in a voice that had a touch of sinister motivation.

There was a large tree trunk that had fallen down, and it looked like a good place for her to be able to sit and still look over what he was doing. She went over to it and sat down a few feet from him.

"Are you going to play with that stupid dam all day?" she asked him.

"It's not stupid," he said to her in a tone defending his hard and crafty work. He stopped what he was doing and just looked at her, sneering. He stood there with sticks in one hand and mud in the other and just stared at her.

"Yes, it is. Wouldn't you rather come over here and sit with me?" she said in a seductive tone.

He paused what he was doing and stood there, thinking for a moment. He wasn't sure if he wanted to stop.

He stopped what he was doing and dropped everything from his hands. He began running the water through his fingers, cleaning them of the mud that was coating his skin. He got up from where he was washing his hands and walked over to the log where she was sitting and sat down next to her.

"Have you ever touched a girl?" she said to him softly.

"Why would I touch a girl?" he replied, not understanding her.

"Would you like to touch me?" she asked him, this time with a twinkle in her eyes, trying to tempt him and relax him at the same time.

He tried to get up without responding to her, but she grabbed him by the shoulder and pulled him back down to his seat.

She reached out to him as he sat there and grabbed his wrist. He resisted her at first, not wanting her to touch him, but then she got more forceful and would not let him pull his hand away.

With his wrist held tight in her grip, she slowly pulled his hand closer to her. As his hand came closer to her, she guided his hand onto her left breast. She felt his hand on her breast, and the feeling made her feel dirty and nasty inside in an instant. Someone else's touch—especially on the part of her that was so private and intimate—immediately made her disgusted.

At that same moment when the feeling of disgust hit her, the boy had begun to squeeze her breast gently in awe of its softness. Then he began to squeeze a little harder, and that was when she unleashed on him. She slapped him so hard that he fell backward over the log that they were sitting on. He landed on his back with his legs sitting across the log above him.

Anne got up from where she was sitting and went around the log where the boy was gasping on the ground for air. His lungs felt as if they had become void of the air that had filled them. He gasped, trying to refill them. Anne stood above the boy, watching him struggle to get air into his lungs. The disgusted look on her face said it all. The boy looked up at her, but he couldn't put together words to speak.

Anne lifted up her right foot, and with all her might, she brought it down onto the boy's stomach. He gasped as she stood above him, looking down at him. As he looked up at her, a smile began to creep onto her face—a smile of satisfaction. She lifted her foot and brought it down on him again, then again and again and again.

When she turned around and walked away, headed toward home, the boy was quiet. He did not move.

Later that night, there was a knock on the door during supper. Her mother got up from the dinner table and went and answered the door as Anne continued to eat her dinner.

When her mother returned to the table, she sat down. She didn't say a word. Her mother did not look at her. Her mother suspected that Anne was behind what had happened this morning, and the fear of her own daughter was evident from that day forward. Two weeks later, Anne-Kay Ruth was in a home for girls.

# CHAPTER 10

## Second Breakfast

A gruff voice spoke to him. It was a voice that had intent. It was a voice that was demanding, and behind that voice was someone who had lived a long life while making those demands, a position in life, and a personality of stone made for complex situations.

His eyes opened slowly, but he did not want them to be seen open. He lay there still, dreading having to move just like last night.

"Your breakfast is on the table," the gruff voice said to him again but quietly. She knew he was awake. He knew that she knew that he was awake.

"We have work to do today. So it's time you get up, get in there, and eat, so we can get busy." But what she actually meant by that was he was going to do stuff while she was going to sit and yell at *Jerry Springer* all day. How you could go from being a nun to being able to watch *Jerry Springer* reruns all day had him wanting to put his fist upside his head again but really hard. He wanted to knock the thought out of his head.

Here he was. He was in the clutches of his very own horror story. He knew he didn't have much time. She was going to be getting mean to him soon if he didn't make a move. The safest thing for him to do would be to wrap himself up in his blanket—by the way, his mom said it would keep him safe—and try to get to the kitchen as quickly as possible.

So he sat up, wrapped himself in the blanket, and looked at right into her eyes. He told her good morning, but he realized, and it only took a second to remember, that she did not want to hear him speak. The sound of his voice was, to her, like his teacher's nails on her chalkboard. His teacher ran her nails down the board when she got really mad in class. It was an awful sound. It made him want to run for the door.

Mrs. Ruth scowled at him in a way that sent chills up his back. If she didn't have such a long and wrinkled face, he wouldn't have been so afraid of her. But the way that she sat there in her chair, it was hard not to want to hide under a rock or something and not come out no matter how bored or uncomfortable he got. He got up and went to the kitchen, but he did think about actually starting to run.

His mom told him that when Mrs. Ruth left being a nun, she married an old man, and he died in this house. *I have to sit at the table of a dead man*, he started thinking to himself. *Do I sit in his chair? Does he still roam the walls of this house?*

It was almost Halloween, and with all the monsters popping up on lawns across town, it had him thinking about all the things that were there, but they didn't want to see: the shadows. All those things that lurked in the shadows, in the silence.

He threw himself down in a chair at the kitchen table that greeted him with not a bowl of oatmeal with a scoop of peanut butter in it, but a bowl of Cheerios that had drunk all his milk, along with two plastic airplanes. Mrs. Ruth said that peanut butter was protein so you had lots of muscle so God could punish the devil out of you. How could you not be puzzled by that irrational mind?

Whenever he had cereal, he liked to be able to take a little drink between bites, maybe with his spoon or with the whole bowl to his face. Instead, his cereal drank all his milk. It was so soggy that you could plant a tree in it. How many times had a man, whom she probably had buried under the piles of leaves that she made him stack all day, sat in the chair that he had to sit in now?

The answer wasn't what he wanted. What he wanted was something else to think about so that he did not have to think about eating what was in front of him. He was stuck. He had to pick up the spoon and start shoveling. That was the only option he had. There were no good options in this house. They were all either bad or really bad. She was not going to let him get away with not eating it, and that was that.

He picked up the spoon and began to rustle in the bowl. *Clink. Clink.* For ten minutes, it went on. It could have been far longer, but who was keeping track? He was too smart to know that she was well aware that he was not eating. He knew that she was just waiting him out. She would rise from her chair soon, and he knew that it would not be a superhero's last stand, it would be the alamo. He would go down like everybody else.

He was no match. She had him by years, size, weight, and meanness. He didn't have much meanness in him to fight her with. So it was going to be—In the middle of his thoughts, he heard a *whap* ring out.

It instantly grabbed his attention. While he was gazing in another place and pretending in his head not to be here and playing with his food, he was unaware of her arrival behind him. She had been standing there for god only knows how long, probably just watching him and growing with anger.

With a three-foot wooden yardstick, she had come down hard onto the bone of his wrist. Not only did it burn his skin and made it sting like all got out, but the bone also took a hard hit. He was instantly in pain. The slap that his mom put on him last night was nothing compared to that. He pulled his wrist into his chest and clutched it. It stung, and it hurt, the bone by far more than the skin.

"God put that food on the table in front of you, so you had better eat it!" she yelled at him resolutely. Her anger was starting to build, and he knew that when she started to get angry, she stayed angry.

"Your mother won't be here until late. That means you got time to get some work done. Do you understand what I'm saying to you, boy?" she said this last part with a much lower tone, and the lower tone was far scarier than the screaming voice.

Billy had to gather himself. He was so mad that he could barely hold back, but all that he could think about was the bone that she had collided perfectly with her stick.

"God didn't put that crap there! You did!" Billy screamed out. He couldn't hold it back. *Bam. There goes my trouble hole*, he thought to himself. He stood as still as a wax museum statue. He was probably as pale. All the blood rushed from his face, and he probably developed a clammy sweat.

For the second time in such a short period of time, he had opened his mouth and had gotten himself in deep. Mrs. Ruth unleashed a slap across his face almost exactly like his mother had done.

When he said trouble hole, it was true. He was in big trouble. He had never attempted to lash out at her like that. He was now in total fear of her as she looked down at him with utter disdain.

Without any time to respond, Mrs. Ruth reached out and clutched him by his left ear. The pain from his wrist was now in competition with his ear. She pulled on it harder, and the pain was brilliant. He sat there at first as she tugged away at it, applying more pressure as he continued to sit in the chair. After he realized that she was not letting up, he began to move in her direction to ease the pain in his protruding ear to keep it from ripping from his skull.

"You little bastard," she yelled out at him, little drops of spit jettisoning from her mouth and onto the side of his face. She pulled his ear harder, directing him closer to her face. "You'll pay for that, Mr. Smart Kid. All you boys are the same, full of that nastiness. You're all the same. You need to be punished. You need to be sent to hell to pay for your sins!" she belted out at him so close to his ear that it left his ear ringing.

He stayed silent, afraid that he would just open his trouble hole and make the situation even worse than it had already gotten. He thought the smartest thing that he could have done at that moment was to run—run and run fast. But he didn't. He stood there as she pulled him close.

He thought the pain in his ear made the pain in his wrist completely disappear. He looked down and noticed that blood had been coming out of his wrist where her yardstick had caught him on the bone and began running down onto the floor.

It was at that point that he realized that his cereal was no longer on the plan for the day. If there was anything good to come out of any of this, it was going to be that he wouldn't have to shovel slop into his face. It would make him sick and want to throw up. There was always a chance of that; it had happened before. It wasn't his first run-in with a bowl of cereal that became a congealed glop.

With no will to fight her, he let her pull him through the kitchen by his ear. It was not slow, and it was not peaceful. She tugged at his ear. He did not know how she did not pull it completely off the side of his head. They made it through the kitchen, both of them going through the doorway at the same time because she had pulled him so close toward her that they were almost one body going through it.

She stopped when they reached the back room where there was a door that was half as tall as the beast who had her grips on his listening hole.

With one hand, she kept a tight grip on his ear; and with the other, she reached for the handle but fought it and him at the same time before she finally unlocked it through all his squirming around.

She pulled it open. When she opened the door, the dank smell hit him and then the smell of dirt and some other nasty smell that was unfamiliar. The dampness and the chilled air did not feel like any place that he would like to be. *The spiders down below will probably be fifty times as big as the one I had contended with upstairs*, he thought to himself as his fear of entering the open door gripped at him. The smell that spilled through the open door was not a pleasant one.

There were four steps that led down to a dirt floor at the base of the stairs, a Michigan basement, and he was staring at it right into the face. Cobwebs extended from one corner of the entrance to the other and in continuous opposite directions. Entering the doorway was only going to attract all the webs to his clothes, hair, and skin; and without doubt, it would be covering his face and getting into his mouth.

She turned on the light with a long string that hung from a bulb that would be the only thing between him and the darkness below. It was supposed to light up the way, but the light was so dim that the only thing that it was lighting up was the stairway to doom.

A shadow at the base of the stairs was where the light ended and the darkness began. *Where the darkness began,* he thought to himself, *and "them bugs,"* like his mom always said, began to crawl up his arms. Then the goose bumps spread to the rest of him. His fear began to take hold as the sounds from down below began to slowly sing in the background. She pulled his ear harder and directed him to the first step.

"Get down there and spread the lime," she said. The hostility in her voice, he knew, was just a speck of salt away from being monumental. "There's a rake, and I'll throw down the bags."

She gave him an aggressive and forceful push, and down the stairs, he went—face-first.

# CHAPTER 11

## Mom's Love for Dad

The helicopter shuddered and banged as it chugged its way through the mountain air. The darkness hid the mountains that clung to the horizon in every direction. He sat on his seat and kept his head from hitting the shaking hull of the aircraft.

His stomach was churning but not because he was hungry but because he was homesick. He could not get it off his mind: her and him and the soon-to-be baby.

Hopefully, he could be there for the birth. He wasn't certain, but he would do anything in his power to be there. Why would a man not want to be there for the birth of his child? How a man could be so squeamish not to watch the birth of their child was beyond him. A man is a man and nothing less. "Put on a pair and pull 'em up" was what he would say.

"Congratulations on the baby, Sergeant," a voice in the next seat said to him over the grumbling blare of the helicopter's engines.

"Thank you, sir," he replied, not knowing if he would actually be heard.

His lieutenant was a solid leader and was a man who was a bit of a mystery. His echoes of quiet left many of the men in fear of him. His way of hastening his men without uttering a word was a sight to behold. The men respected him, and Billy had become a close friend through all of their tribulations and conflicts fought side by side. Both lead each other and the men together. Billy knew that leadership is not always leadership. The man sitting beside him with proudly worn lieutenant's bars was as reliable as they could get.

"Have you come up with names yet?" the lieutenant asked out to him.

"Adam if it's a boy, and Isabelle if it's a girl," he screamed back at him.

"Get it done on the ground, Sergeant," the lieutenant nodded to him, and the two of them had a silent agreement: to make it back onto the chopper when it was over, along with everybody else, and look after each other in the process. The two of them had a special bond as they looked over the aircraft full of men. They watched each other's backs. It had just become a part of the drill.

September eleventh was a long time ago, and he didn't remember seeing it unfold live like so many people much older than him did. He was too young, but there was one thing that he did not forget: the horror that appeared on his mother's and his father's faces.

He watched them in fear, and he saw their anguish. A young child is very perceptive of his/her mom and dad, and parents are very impressionable. A child's parents are the focus of their world. If a child's parents become a part of their lives, the child can tell if something is wrong. Why is Mommy so sad? Why are you crying, Daddy? Those were the questions that he had.

As he got older and he learned more, he became a Boy Scout and participated in school sports along with keeping his grades higher than all but a few of the kids in his graduating class. When he graduated from high school, his parents were there, and they couldn't have been prouder. That day was the second time that he had seen his father cry.

He joined the military weeks after he graduated and days after he turned eighteen. His father saw him off on the bus to boot camp, but his mother said goodbye at the front door. She couldn't take seeing him off on the bus. She said it was slow sadness. She wanted the sadness to turn the corner down the street, not sit and listen to the engine run for thirty minutes before he left.

He met Brandy on one of his first leaves home. The two of them fell in love, and she had been his whole world for over the last eight years. Both of them were ready to have children and settle down and have a nice family life together.

He had spent fifteen months overseas over the last two years, but it had only seemed to make their relationship prosper. He had been in the military since high school, but he felt he really needed to move on. She liked to mail letters with plastic ants in the envelopes to keep his attention while he read. At the chow hall, the ants always brought a look or two. It was just one of the little things she did.

She was a rock during his deployments. She kept in contact the best she could, and she started to make our house feel like a home. She worked two jobs, not only to fill her days but also to get their home life in order.

His deployments were very dangerous, and she knew it. She knew what it was he did, but she had faith. She believed that he would come home to her and now the baby, and he always did. He never so much as had a scratch on him. He had a couple of new scars that she did not know the origin of, and he was not open to telling her the truth behind them. The truth was that they were there and there for a good reason. That was his reasoning for not just coming up with the answer.

She watched as he put his hand on her belly and talked to his unborn child. As she watched him, she knew that he would be a wonderful father. It was the baby that had changed his thinking about being a soldier. Brandy had guilt though about the pregnancy. She felt guilty that she was pulling him away from something that he believed in. But a child would want him home. A child would need him home.

He was a brilliant man, and she knew that. The military was not what she believed he should be doing with his life, but she knew that the importance of it made him who he was. He wanted to be known and to be remembered as a good man. His parents instilled pride in him and the importance of education. He used that advice and became the best man that any woman could want.

They married the last time he went home on leave. It was a big wedding, and he was so grateful that his parents were there to help Brandy with taking care of all the wedding arrangements. He was of no help when it came to the wedding, but the two-week honeymoon after was all his doing. He arranged everything, two weeks in Hawaii.

He could close his eyes now and see her beautiful face. Her eyes glowed from happiness. The ocean sunset was in the background as he looked with awe at her beauty. He pictured it in his mind as if it were yesterday. He had loved and cherished every moment of their time together. They hadn't had much time together lately, but what they had had had been better than anything he could have imagined.

They would make love for hours and walk on the beach late at night. The moon lit up the dark horizon and gave shadows to the waves as they lapped the shoreline. They were happy. They were going to be a family.

He felt the shutters of the helicopter as he thought of home, knowing they were almost there. He reached into his breast pocket and pulled a picture of her out of his pocket. He kissed it. "I love you, Brandy Wine." He put the picture back into his pocket.

The aircraft started to descend, and as they got closer to the ground, little pings began to sound off as rounds began to ricochet off the sides of the helicopter. All the men got to their feet, knowing the urgency now that it was known that they were here.

The big bulky helicopter wheels sat down into the sand, and the large back door began to go down. Men started making their way out the back of the aircraft. He was next. He stuck his left foot out and began to run, his lieutenant right on his heels. Bullets rang out, and even the rotors couldn't drown out the gunfire.

He made it five feet when a round that was probably just a random lucky shot caught him in the throat, and his body fell lifeless to the ground. The lieutenant came to his aid as the rotors of the aircraft began to lift off the ground above him. He rolled his body over, and when he did so, he noticed the life in his eyes was gone. The lieutenant hesitated for a moment to gather a breath.

"Wagner is down. I repeat, Wagner is down," the lieutenant said into his mouthpiece. The round had severed Billy's spine at the base of his skull. His death was instant.

*****

It was seven o'clock in the evening in Michigan when the door-bell rang. Brandy was surprised to hear it ring because nothing in the place actually worked. Base housing was not bad, but getting anything fixed was just a dream.

She got up from the couch where she was watching her evening episode of *Jeopardy*. She was a routine kind of girl, and the consistency helped to keep her from missing her man. She walked over to the front door and opened it.

There were two men standing at the door. She hesitated when she saw them and became very still. She did not say a word. A very sickening feeling began to expand in her stomach. Within a matter of moments, that sickening feeling in her stomach had spread to her whole body. It was getting harder for her to stand. The two men at the door realized what was about to occur and reached out for her before she collapsed. She came out of her daze as the two men looked down at her.

"Is there someone we can call, Mrs. Wagner?" she heard a voice say, but it was like in a tunnel. The voice seemed so far away. She listened, and the voice spoke again.

She sat up and pressured the men to leave. She had a desperate desire to be alone suddenly. As the door closed behind them as they left, she looked down at the stomach that was well on its way to birthing. She put both of her hands on her belly to touch the child that he had given her.

"Oh, Billy," she said quietly and gently with a crackle in her voice. She sat and cried for hours.

# CHAPTER 12

## Audrey Copes

The alarm went off at 5:50 a.m., and Audrey McCallister reached over and grabbed the phone off the table next to her bed. "I'm up," she said to the phone as she picked it up and turned it off. She set the phone down and stretched, getting that good feeling of the back muscles stretching.

*Amazing what a good night's sleep does for you*, she thought to herself. She was so tired when she got home from work the other night that she promised herself that she would go to bed early last night. She did, and it was well worth it. She felt like a million bucks.

She had three days out of the week that she worked fifteen-hour days, and sometimes, by the middle of the week, she was done for. Two of those fifteen-hour days were on the weekends. That didn't include nights that she had to play pool. Sometimes, she would go up to the Billiards and shoot for a little while, but lately, it seemed that it had all been catching up to her.

For the last two years, she had been working her ass off. She worked on the truck and at the waste site, sometimes fifty or sixty hours a week. At the bar, she basically was working for tips. She could make a good three or four hundred on the weekends, and she saved all that money. She won a pool tournament last month and made five thousand dollars in one weekend, and that boosted her savings account well.

She threw off the covers and put her feet on the floor, hoping that her slippers were there. The floor got so cold in this dump. She considered herself lucky just to have the heat that she had. She never understood why the house was 78 degrees all day, but the floors always felt like icicles. Don't even get her started about the dishwasher that didn't work, the water that never got warm, and the stupid ass washer downstairs that didn't work.

She hated getting up in the mornings. Mornings were always such a drag, and not only that, but it was also unfortunate for anybody who ran into her because she was a real bear in the mornings, especially before that all-important first cup of coffee in the morning.

Is it a psychological thing with the coffee? Or does caffeine really give you coping skills? That was a question she had and an answer she really didn't give a s———it about especially at this moment.

She had exactly thirty minutes to shower, dress, eat, and get out the door, grabbing a cup of coffee if she had time. But if she didn't have time, boy, there would be hell to pay.

She was dreading today, and she was excited all at the same time. It was a little difficult to be excited though with the day from hell ahead of her.

It got really difficult for her to go from stressful situations, like today was going to be, to a situation where she had to be relaxed, playing pool. For some reason, she just couldn't turn it off. It was going to be a long day, and she knew it. Turning it off after spending the day with Jimmy the a———hole was going to be tough.

Her day was going to start off with going down to Howard Waste Services and punching in by seven after she went through the drive-through and got herself the largest cup of coffee she could find, of course. Then she had to go find Jimmy who would probably be in the breakroom.

It seemed that any time she had to try and find him, that was where he would be. The breakroom was kind of the catchall hole for guy talk and the bull that they slung around. For her, it was kind of a hornet's nest, so she would just be somewhere else without a doubt. The guys all hung out there, and she sure wasn't one of them. That and she was quite sure that business went on in there that she had no interest in knowing anything about.

The only thing Jimmy wanted to do was eat, but he was as skinny as a beanpole. However, Jimmy might be as skinny as a beanpole, but Jimmy was dangerous, and she was very careful not to forget that.

Jimmy had been slinging garbage for his father since he was in his early teens, and he was physically intimidating. His tattoos had a little bit to do with that. He had them running up both arms to his shoulders and then up the side of his neck to just under his ears.

The biggest problem with Jimmy was that the guy was just plain and simply crazy out of his mind. That was one of the biggest problems with Jimmy. She was just happy to not have to be around the guy, pretty simple. When God went to the store to get supplies to make Jimmy, he for sure forgot to get marbles.

Jimmy had a really good temper too, and his fuse was short. It didn't matter what kind of mood he was in. He would just flip a switch, and it could get bad. He had a loose screw somewhere. She had seen him beat up at least three guys in the last two years. Yes, that was how long she had been putting up with his stupid ass.

Jimmy was such a disgusting slob and never showered either. Let me tell you that if you do a job and you work around garbage all day? You stink like garbage. Do you know what a sewer smells like? That was what Jimmy smells like half the time, s——it you not.

Jimmy would throw on trousers in the john after work and go for a drink out the door. It would really suck to be the one who had to serve him drinks after work. But she did feel worse for the person who had the nerve to tell him that. He would probably shoot them.

Ever since the first day that she had started working there, he was always trying to get her to go out with her. The big problem she had with that was that he was always wanting to go to either his house or hers, and you could only guess what for. He was obsessed with her, and it absolutely drove her crazy. That and all his nasty and totally s——itty comments made her want to puke. It was nonstop and relentless.

She absolutely hated sitting up front in the truck with him. She put earbuds in and cranked the music so she couldn't hear him, and he absolutely flipped out on her. There came a point that you had to say enough is enough, but with Jimmy, that didn't exactly work.

He was nasty and mean. He wasn't exactly one of those guys who you tried to put your chest out and stand your ground. If you did, you were likely to get to see the really bad side of him.

Audrey was really looking forward to tonight after work. She was hoping that they would hopefully be able to get through their route by seven tonight so that she could make it to the pool tournament by nine.

She always wondered why they held the damn tournaments so late. She thought it had something to do with maybe wanting to get the players a little loosened up. Ha ha. She would never drink, especially during a tournament. It was bad enough that she had to deal with the other players when they decided to get lit up. Usually, the players were sober, especially the women players.

She started playing pool when she was really young. Both of her parents were pool players. That was how they met and supposedly fell in love and got married. Then she came along, and they both went their separate ways. The only thing that they had in common after that was that they were both alcoholics.

She got bounced back and forth from one drunk parent to the next. It was like living in two totally different but totally dysfunctional homes. She couldn't, for a while, remember which dysfunction belonged to which family.

Her mom dealt with her alcoholism every day on her own. She tried to avoid her because she spiraled down too far, and now they just couldn't get along. Her father died of liver failure at fifty-two because he wouldn't give up drinking to get a liver. She just couldn't watch her mother do the exact same thing. Her mother's favorite tagline was "If I was grateful, I wouldn't be drunk."

She tried telling her mom how bad it made her feel when she said that, but she just either didn't care or didn't understand. She just didn't want to hear it from her, so she kept her distance.

Needless to say, she didn't drink, and she didn't like alcohol. If it wasn't for the pool playing, she would never be in the places that she found herself in. Other than work and pool, she bartend a few nights a week just for a little extra money, once again surrounded by alcohol. She despised it, yet she might as well be tilting people's heads back and pouring it right on in there. "Come on, tilt 'em back for me," that was what she told them at the bar. "Tilt them back!"

Part of her was okay with what had been going on in her life. She got her own place, she got work, and she had a hobby. Hey, life wasn't bad. But part of her was missing something. She just had this feeling that there was something better for her out there, almost like she had a calling.

The only problem was that she was not really good at anything. She played pool, and she was good, but she was no prodigy. She could barely do her own laundry. Her mom and dad didn't exactly fill her full of faith in herself. Watching a couple of drunks when you were growing up was a good recipe to land flat on your face when you got older.

Sometimes, the emotional up and down kind of forgets you on the upswing. When that happens, you stay down sometimes. That was where she was at: on the down. As a woman, you get used to having the ups and downs. It's just a part of life. She couldn't speak for all women, but for her, it was true.

She had no ties here other than her mom, but that relationship was so far in the shitter that there was no point in even trying. She was thinking of maybe going to the Upper Peninsula, maybe getting herself a little place on Lake Superior, waking up every morning and taking in a Pictured Rocks view. A girl could dream, couldn't she? She had been putting aside a little bit of money here and there, so a change of scenery was definitely not out of the question. She thought about moving up there all the time, but she guessed she just didn't have the guts. That and she didn't want to go alone.

She got herself up out of bed and made her way to the shower. She went in and started the shower because it took about ten minutes for the water to make it up to the third floor of the building. She took off her pajama top and her panties and hung them on the hook on the door. Having things on the floor was a pet peeve of hers, and in her own home, it was worse. She could almost be obsessive-compulsive with some things.

She stood there naked and stared at herself in the mirror. She liked the look of her body. She did not have a birthmark or any other disfigurement to her skin. It was almost perfectly uniform on her whole body.

She was a twenty-one-year-old woman whose body was probably now as of this moment as good as it was ever going to get. From here on out, it was downhill. *Jimmy would just love to see the view that I'm seeing now*, she thought to herself.

Jimmy was the biggest piece of s———it she had ever seen, and all the years that she spent playing pool in bars and like establishments, he was the worst she had ever come across. Jimmy was the son of the owner of Howard Waste Services, and there was a really good reason why he drove a garbage truck.

The guy was always in so much trouble. He liked trouble just to like trouble. So his daddy kept him behind the wheel of a garbage truck to keep him out of trouble. She just thought to herself, *What if he decides to go off the rail with a garbage truck under his ass? Good god, I can only imagine the damage he could do*, she thought.

He blew up one of the police cars a couple of towns over. He was never charged for it, but it was spread quietly, his trip to a couple of towns that night. He flat-out admitted it to her without doing so in so many words that would get him into trouble. But she didn't doubt it for a second.

His dumbass just got arrested in the town of Byron about a year ago. His daddy had gotten him out of trouble god only knows how many times. Half the profit from his daddy's company probably went to keeping Jimmy out of jail.

Anyway, he came to find out somebody had thrown a Molotov cocktail at one of their cars one night, and it was a total loss. So he got his revenge. That was not even the bad part about Jimmy. The bad part was that he had a loose screw, and when it meant he had a loose screw, that was exactly what it meant. He was a criminal at heart, and no garbage truck job or any other kind of job was going to change that.

She got into the shower and washed and let the hot water just flow down her back. She loved taking showers in the morning because it woke her up, but she always had to shower after work, so if she did both, it would become a third job. She laughed to herself. She was in a good mood this morning. Kicking some ass in the pool tournament would be her big focus today. "Stay positive," she said to herself out loud. Being out on the truck with Jimmy all day today was going to make that a herculean task.

# CHAPTER 13

## The Dark

Billy landed with his arms sticking straight out and his legs sprawled when she threw him headfirst into the hole. A cloud of dust shot out from underneath him when he landed. He had a face full of dirt, and the cobwebs that had blocked the entrance were now all over him and his face. His hair felt full of cobwebs. They clung to him like Saran Wrap.

His clothes were covered with dirt, and a creepy feeling shot through his body as the feeling of the silk touching his skin touched off the nerves on every exposed inch of skin that was not clothed.

The first reaction he had was to start clawing at his skin and at his head and at his face to remove any trace of silk that clung to him, but as he did so, he just made the situation worse. He just continued to spread the dirt and the webs from one part of his body to another. His face now had dirt and webs spread all over it, and his hair was matted, and there was dirt in his hair.

He looked around, but the light at the top of the stairs offered him little help. He stood there at the base of the stairs and wondered what was down here in the crawl space with him. After she swung the door shut and put the hasp back on, the light went with her.

Now he was down here in the quiet with only a tiny light bulb filament between him and absolute darkness. He heard her footsteps trail off in the dark, and then there was only quiet. Maybe his eyes will get used to the dark, and he will be able to see. Or maybe he didn't want to see.

Whatever it was out there making tiny sounds that seemed to get magnified, he didn't want to know about. He was just hoping that they would stay away. He could hear noises, but he could not see nor could he imagine what it was that was keeping him company in the dark.

He dragged the bags of lime over to the middle of the floor. He could hear something moving, but he could not tell from which direction the noise was coming.

He grabbed the shovel off the floor and stabbed at the first bag in an attempt to split it open. Cobwebs kept hitting him in the face as he moved in any direction. They were attached to everything, and he constantly had to run his sleeve across his face to clear his eyes and the webs from his face.

His first strike at the bag worked, and the powder began to spill out onto the floor. He stopped and listened for what continued to make noise, but he could not tell from what direction the noise kept coming from.

For what seemed like forever, he spread the powder out, slowly venturing from the center of the room as he continued to spread the powder. The room seemed large, but he could not see the outer walls.

The light at the top of the stairs was supposed to help him see, but it did not go any further than the stairs. All the time he was working, something had continued to rustle somewhere out of sight. He was covered in cobwebs and dirt. Now that he was close to being done, he had added a layer of dust from the powder that he had been continuously spreading.

All of a sudden, something landed on his back. He didn't know what it was or where it came from, but he could feel small claws that had penetrated his shirt and forced their way into his skin. It began to crawl on his shoulders in a desperate attempt to get away from him, but it just ended up running back and forth on his shoulders as he began to try to shake it off.

His arms and hands went right to his shoulders to get off what had just landed on his back. His feet began running in the direction of the stairs to make his way out of this hellhole.

He ran up the stairs, flailing at his shoulders to get off what was on him, and the door burst open when he reached the top of the stairs. In the process of going through the door, he ran directly into the stomach of Mrs. Ruth. She was in the process of opening the door at the same time he was racing toward the door. She opened the door to see what the explosion of noise coming from the basement was all about.

As he went through the doorway at the top of the stairs, he collided with her large body, and his momentum carried him into her, forcing her backward and him forward, taking them both back into free fall.

He landed on top of her when she fell backward. She was as stunned as him to have him on top of her. She made moaning sounds from the impact of her hitting the ground and him landing on top of her.

With very little effort, she launched him off her, and she began to scream profanities at him. She made her way to her knees as he lay on the floor, reeling from the pain in his legs from hitting them on the lips of the stairs as he made his way to the top.

The dirt from the basement covered his face, and he looked like he had just come out of a coal mine. When she made it to her feet, she looked down at him and grabbed his arm close to his shoulder. She yanked on it, pulling him to his feet. He stared down at the floor and just wanted his mom.

# CHAPTER 14

## A New Home

Anne found a new home, and it was more comfortable than the life she had been living. She hated her mother, and her father was not much better. There was a different kind of structure in her life, and among the nuns, she prospered. For over the next forty years, she would become woven into the fabric of the church. It became all she was. She prospered and became content.

With a lot of hard work and a lot of jostling, Sister Ruth became Reverend Mother for the school for boys. With this position, she had turned the home into the most disciplined that it had ever been in its lifetime.

The Reverend Mother had no need to fight with an angry father or a belligerent mother here at the home for boys. There were none of them checking in on these classrooms.

It was eight years after her attainment of Reverend Mother that the unthinkable happened, unthinkable to Sister Ruth anyway. Allegations of abuse had swirled in the air among the sisters and among the staff of the school.

No cases had been proven due to the tight-lipped inner circle protectors of everything discreet within those walls of the leadership. There were children in need of nighttime care, and some injuries required long-term care. None of it ever came to light even after her departure as the head of the school. One night, a boy under Sister

Ruth's care died. She had been disciplined and had been forced to give up her life's achievements.

Life is about cruelty, suffering cruelty. Life is about surviving cruelty. Without cruelty, we cannot have character. Without character, we cannot judge those who shall go before God to relinquish their sins or be thrown into the depths of hell. It was what Anne believed. She believed that cruelty prepared you to be with God. That is what Jesus suffered—she always professed.

She had nothing when she left the church. She agreed to marry to solve several problems: financial security and her belief in being married. She needed to acquire one to have the other.

She married shortly after leaving the church, and she cared for her husband for over a dozen years until his death. For those dozen years, she had unleashed an unpleasantness that no man could comprehend.

She was bitter with him to the point that her only escape was the death of the man whom she had come to loathe more than any other. His constant needs had tested her resolve to not rest a pillow on his face and pull the ends that he would, in a matter of minutes, meet the devil that was most likely to visit him upon his death.

She had started her life off mean, and she carried that with her always. She would until the moment that she passed her last breath, and with her last breath, her past would reach out to her and grab her and pull her close to unleash the demon that had a true grip on her soul.

Her husband's naked body filled her with disgust as she washed it before he was laid to rest. She cursed it for all that it was worth. She married him and roamed the halls of a home where a physical touch would only be that of one by accident.

There was no marriage consummation. There was an agreement, and then there was distance. She was deemed a caregiver; she deemed it her deliverance from a tyrannical society within the church that she had begun to loathe.

She could no longer force her will upon anybody, and that left her empty inside. It was only the crippled man who had her focus, and for a dozen long years, she made him into a silent and bitter old man. She concocted a home hierarchy, him being the one to desire something and either receive it or not would be at her discretion.

It was the children who gave her purpose as Reverend Mother. That purpose however became pain and brutality and empty dreams for youth that were embedded in a place that had become a horror.

Her anger became less controllable as the years passed from one to the next. The past had begun to gnaw on her like a really big dog with a really big bone. The past had begun to haunt her.

# CHAPTER 15

## Billy Wants to Cry

Billy just wanted to cry. He wanted to just start balling his eyes out and not stop until his mother got here to pick him up. Sometimes, a really good cry can just release all the tension. A good cry can take you away from the reality of it all, like being in a mist with the torture queen. Maybe that was what he really needed. Billy just needed to get away from it all right now if at all possible.

He had gotten close to crying, but he thought of his mother. He didn't want her to be disappointed in him. He looked up to her in a way. His mom was strong, and he knew it. When he was having a really hard time, he missed her.

When he was really young, his mother missed his dad, and Grandma told him that it was because she was heartsick. Even a child could understand that. When he and his mom moved back downstate, it was like she had a new life. Maybe it was Grandma and Grandpa that had reminded her every day of what she had lost.

His mom said that his dad looked like his dad. That was what worried him most, disappointing his mother. He had seen her struggle and had seen her work hard and take care of him. She was the greatest mom a kid could ask for even if she wasn't perfect.

His mom would show him pictures of his dad, but it was hard for her to look at them, and he knew that. But she never wanted to talk about Dad. She would walk around the subject like a donkey in a grain mill. She didn't have very many pictures, but Grandma and

Grandpa would always give her framed pictures of the family as gifts. We were a really small family, but we did have each other.

The pain had all started to come to him at once. There would be bruises and cuts and nicks and who knows what all else when Anne was through with him. Just about the only thing that didn't hurt him at this moment was his teeth. His hair didn't hurt but that was probably because it was full of dirt and cobwebs.

He just wanted to unleash a cry out and yell for his mother and will her here to smash the beast that had such a tight grip on his arm that it had gone numb. He was in a real struggle. His fear had gripped him last night. His fear had been gripping him this morning. But now, it was being tired that he felt most. The huge woman who had a death grip on his arm no longer looked like a towering beast over him. His anger had pushed aside all the other emotions that he had been feeling.

When the rat was on his back, he had been taken to a place with his emotions that he didn't think that he could ever be that scared again.

She yanked at him. He yanked back from her. She pulled, and he pulled. *I would not dare swing out, but maybe I should*, he thought. With his left arm in a viselike grip, it was of no use to him. With his right, he came around as hard and as fast as he could with it. The desperate attempt to free his arm was launched.

When his fist hit her arm, it just bounced off. She saw the swing, and she saw his fist coming. But when it reached her, she felt nothing, not even a sting. He was a weakling, a weak little insufferable boy. Vanquishing them all would be her preference, but God will sort it all out for her. He unleashed a fury of hits at her, but it did no good. They neither caused her pain nor gave her pause to release his arm.

The two of them struggled for almost ten minutes. He was trying to keep her from pulling him; she was trying to drag him into the kitchen. They both began to tire. She pulled him, and after he tired, she began to drag him.

He had no more fight in him; he was tired. She dragged him through the house, but they stopped at the front door. She unlatched the heavy front door and pulled it open.

"Get out there and clean up those leaves," she said to him. She could barely say the words. She was tired too. She was probably more tired than him, but he didn't know that. What he saw was an angry woman who was just an inch away from killing him. He did not rule that out. It was a possibility. *She is crazy after all*, he thought to himself.

# CHAPTER 16

## Gilligan's Island

*Gilligan's Island* played on the television as the monitors beeped out their continuous chirping sounds, and the breathing machine gave out its own continuous sucking sound. Dean Wagner lies in bed, not moving and unconscious. His wife, Barb, was by his side. The two of them resembled Mr. and Mrs. Howell on *Gilligan's Island,* but only in looks. They were by far from wealthy that made the two of them famous in the show.

It was his favorite program, and while he had been home in hospice, she had kept it on a continuous loop so that if he awoke, he would be able to hear or see it. She tried to make him as comfortable as possible in his last days with her, and if there was something that she could do for him, she would. She would miss him. He would be buried right next to his son soon. The thought of that broke her heart.

She was going to be alone, and she did not know what to do with that. She had been with Dean for so long, and their lives were so entangled she had no idea what she was going to do. Should she sell everything and travel? Should she sit home all day and wait for the grim reaper to come for her too?

The two of them made that decision when their son was killed to get the three plots. She was now living with the reality that two of the three would be filled in just a matter of a couple of years. She was hoping that the third plot that was hers would stay empty for at least a little while longer.

Dean and her had been married for forty-two years, and she believed in her heart that not a single one of those years was a bad year. They had had such a wonderful life together. They never had the types of problems that a lot of couples have: infidelity and all that other stuff. She was so happy that they had never had those types of problems.

As two married people, they were always content with each other and what they had. She could never understand what made people do the things they do. When you marry someone, that is what your life becomes: one person living the life of two. It was always about working together with the two of them, and they figured that that was what helped to make their marriage worked.

She had never worked outside the home in any of the forty-two years that they had been married. He had built an electrical business from a pair of wire cutters and a desire to succeed, to have a very successful business, allowing the two of them to retire and come up to live in Traverse City, where the view of lake Michigan could be taken in every morning.

He had hoped to be able to hand the business down to Billy and Brandy when he retired, but it didn't work out that way. Billy was killed shortly before he was scheduled to be released from the military, and his father, Dean, was diagnosed with cancer, not long after Billy's death.

Here they were years later still battling the same battle. The sadness that they both felt when their son died had never gone away. It seemed as if the sadness lingered in the house like a bad smell. When Dean was diagnosed with cancer, Barb focused on keeping him alive as long as she could. For years, she helped him fight.

They beat cancer the first time, and she figured she could help him beat it the second time when it came back. But his cancer went from bad to worse in a very short period of time. During his first bout with cancer, Brandy and little Billy were there to help him, and they were part of the support system that helped him to beat it. But after Brandy took Billy and moved back downstate, she had been alone. The house was too quiet.

Brandy stayed with them for three years after Billy had died, and Barb and Dean got used to having her and Billy Junior with them every day. Brandy struggled though. She was struck by something that a lot of people don't go through.

She took the death of her husband really hard especially because she was pregnant when he was killed. For six months after Billy was born, she never left the house. She became almost a hermit. She was quiet. At times, she had nightmares; and sometimes, she would distance herself completely. It was difficult for Billy to feel the distance from his mother.

Fortunately for Billy, he had grandparents to look after him. Barb thought that the depression got the best of Brandy in the worst way. After Barb saw what she went through, she saw Brandy in a very different light. She had a lot of guilt about Brandy. She treated Brandy badly for years while she was married to her son. She realized it, but it was too bad that it was the death of her son that forced her to see the truth. *The blinders that people put up sometimes can be really unhealthy*, she thought.

She thought that that was the reason that she moved back downstate. Brandy didn't have any family except for Dean and Barb, but she wanted to try to be independent. Barb just wished she hadn't moved so far away.

She picked up the phone and dialed Brandy's number for the third time today. She wasn't sure if Dean was going to make it through the night, and she wanted Brandy to know. Little Billy was not going to take the news very well. He was very close to his grandfather.

His grandfather became his father the first few years of his life until his mother started to recover from her breakdown. But during that time, the two of them were very close. They spent a lot of time together, but Dean's cancer had got to the point that he couldn't get around too easily. It was harder for him to chase around a two-year-old. He just didn't have the strength.

Dean had recovered from his first bout with cancer, but it was the colon cancer that paid a visit and was never going to leave, not until it ate him alive and left him a ninety-pound man just waiting for the end to come.

Barb was glad for him, in a way, that the end was near. He had suffered many years of pain, and it was time for him to get some relief from all this. All the machines endlessly beep their way into subconsciousness. She might never be able to get that beeping sound out of her head. It was painful for her to think about.

After the sixth ring on the telephone, she set the phone back on the table and sat on the edge of her husband's bed and took his hand into hers.

# CHAPTER 17

## Brandy Needs a Vacation

Brandy was ready for a vacation. With everything that had been going on lately, she was due. But a vacation was a long way down the road for sure. With all that was going, she just felt like she was being torn in a hundred different directions.

Billy was a great kid, and she couldn't ask for a better son, but she was at her wits end. However, all kids bring with them a degree of stress. That's just the way that it is, and they need your time. She tried to give him as much time as she could, but even that was in short supply. So pressure and time was something that was not on her side. "Hmm, I should have diamonds coming out of my ass then," she said to herself with a smile on her face.

Between work and Billy and now Grandma Barb, Brandy was stretched pretty thin. Barb had her hands full, and she felt bad that she wasn't there for her, but living so far away and having a car that she had to worry about getting to work with every day made that kind of difficult.

Taking Billy to Mrs. Ruth's had started to become a real big hassle. Not only was it far out of the way but she was also having a hard time getting to work on time.

But this morning was an entirely different story. This morning was out of an acorn's a——hole. This morning was the big kicker. This morning was luck getting s——it out by a leprechaun. She stopped at the store last night on her way home, and one of the things that she had put on her list at the store was a pregnancy test.

It wasn't a bad thing to her, but it was horrible timing, but the possibility of being pregnant was kind of exciting. She had started seeing Alex about three months ago. Because Billy was really sensitive about the subject of his father, she had been worried about telling him.

She knew he would be happy when she would tell him, so at least that was a good thing. Telling Billy about Alex and about having a brother or sister, that was something else altogether. She was just sitting there, thinking about all the life situations that we go through in a lifetime, and we all wonder why we get gray hair as we grow older. *Me, personally, I should have a complete head of gray hair*, she thought to herself.

One of her biggest concerns was getting Billy up to see his grandfather. Those two had spent so much time together when he was growing up, and Dean's health went downhill so quickly that they hadn't been able to get up there. She didn't want to have to put that on Billy right now too. He was going to have a lot coming at him hard and fast in the near future, and she did not envy him for having to take all that in. Her and Billy could get by, and that was what mattered.

# CHAPTER 18

## I Don't Do Garbage

She exited her apartment after she finished getting all the stuff she could carry. Living on the third floor, she tried to carry as much as she could. After she got her hands full and closed the door, she grabbed the garbage to drop it off in the dumpster on her way out the door.

She planned to stop and get a coffee at the shop, but if they were busy, she was going to have to skip it. Somehow, she had managed to make herself late for work. That was another thing that she wasn't great at, getting to work on time.

She exited the front door of the building and made her way around to the side of the building where the dumpster was. She threw the bag of garbage into the dumpster and made her way to the back of the parking lot where her car was usually always parked.

As she unlocked her car door, Jimmy watched her from two blocks away. A field of knee high grass shielded him from view. His binoculars were frozen into place as he savagely gazed into the lens pieces. She just did it for him. He had to have her. She was his.

"I don't know how anybody thinks that I can go without having her," he said to himself as he continued to look through the binoculars until she started her car and sped out of the parking lot. He put away the binoculars and started his car. He reached under the front seat and pulled out the .38 special that he had sitting under the seat.

He checked it to see if it was loaded and set it on the front seat next to him.

Audrey parked her car in the waste management parking lot and gathered her supplies for the day. Jimmy always liked to stop and buy s——it all day, but she hated making stops during the day. She just wanted to do the route and get back to the garage, but he always had to waste time.

She went to the breakroom where Jimmy usually was, but he was not there. She glanced around to take a second look; she was actually surprised that he wasn't there. She walked out into the big bay where a bunch of trucks sat quietly. They were all waiting to erupt with sound at any moment.

She went to her truck and opened the passenger seat and put all her stuff under the seat so it didn't slide around. She leaned over to look under the seat to make sure that it was all nice and snug.

Suddenly, she could feel hands coming around her hips and then a big tug backward. Jimmy had come up quietly behind her and had thrust himself into her. She was instantly infuriated. She wished she had a pool stick so that she could wrap it around this a——hole's face. She swung around and pushed him hard into the side of the truck.

"Don't ever touch me again!" she screamed out at him loud enough so that if anyone was around, they would hear her say it.

Jimmy was furious, and the playful smile that he had on his face was gone. He didn't speak; he just stared at her. All the while that he stood silently, the look on his face became one of extreme agitation. *Did this b——tch just push me?* he thought to himself. He stepped forward slowly as Audrey stood motionless. She had no intentions of showing any fear.

However, Audrey knew at that moment that she had pushed Jimmy backward into the truck that she might have made a huge mistake. Jimmy was one of those guys that could go off the handle with only a tiny push. She had seen him lose it on occasion and always feared being on the other end of Jimmy's anger. Now here she was, and that was exactly what he was—angry.

"Okay, okay," he said as he began to walk toward her. He slowly closed the gap between the two of them. When he got about a foot away from her, he stopped and looked into her eyes. He could sense her fear. He could smell the fear that flowed through her veins and pulsed from the pores of her skin. He looked into her eyes.

In one swift and instantaneous motion, he grabbed her hard in one big fistful of the coveralls that she had put on. The whole chest of her coveralls became scrunched up as it became balled up in one big fist of Jimmy's. He pulled her face close to his as he spun her around and slammed her hard against the side of the truck.

"I'm going to have you one way or the other, you little b——tch, and I'm going to make you like it. Do you understand?" Jimmy was silent and waited for a response as he held her tightly against the truck. He looked into her eyes, shifting from one to the other. He waited, but she said nothing. He pushed her harder into the truck, hoping that maybe it would spur her into saying something. His curiosity grew as she stared back at him and stayed silent.

Then a big smile began to come across her face. He saw the smile start to appear, so he started to smile in reply.

"I don't do garbage," Audrey said to him with disdain in her voice.

The smile on Jimmy's face disappeared as he began to squeeze the front of her coveralls. His anger was building, and he was just about ready to punch her right in her face.

"Cut that s——it out!" a voice screamed out from across the garage.

Jimmy began to let her go slowly as the pressure of the truck against her back began to ease. "This isn't over, you little b——tch," he said as he released the front of her coveralls. She was so tall that she was almost eye to eye with him. He looked down into her eyes, but she stayed silent. He was trying to intimidate her, and she knew it, but she was unwilling to give into him. His anger was pulsing in his veins, and Audrey could see his anger bulging on the sides of his neck. This was the moment when her fear was maxed out. She was stressed, but she refused to show it.

That moment was the first time she thought of quitting and walking out the door. She had spent two years putting up with the guys who worked there. The first few months working around, all the guys there were tough; but eventually, she had earned their respect. Because of that, she didn't ask for help from anyone unless it was absolutely necessary, and that wasn't that often.

Being the only girl working here, she had to put up with some s——it; but up to this point, it wasn't anything that she couldn't handle. But this situation had really struck a nerve with her. This was something else entirely, and she didn't think that going forward with this job was an option. *The money is good, but it isn't that good*, she thought to herself.

Jimmy turned and started to walk away. He did not stop or turn around to look at her as he walked toward the back of the truck and turned out of sight. She felt relief as she took a breath and tried to compose herself and get her nerves to stop sending signals to her hand to shake away.

Audrey could feel herself needing to pee and needing to pee sometime really soon. She could feel the fear that had gripped her start to ease. Her thoughts turned to having to drive with him all day. *How is this going to work?* she thought. *Is he going to kill me and I'll end up in the back of my own garbage truck today?* She thought the questions, but somehow, she got the feeling that she might not be all that far from the truth in asking the question.

The front of the cab was quiet when they both got up and into the truck. Jimmy had been waiting for her while she went to the bathroom to relieve the pressure in several different ways. Getting away from him for a few minutes allowed her to calm her nerves just a little.

She didn't say a word, and neither did he. The big truck roared to life, and the large sound seemed to take away the pressure that came between the silence of two people refusing to be the first to speak. Audrey didn't want the ice to be broken between the two of them. Audrey wanted a ten-feet-wide sheet of ice between the two of them.

# CHAPTER 19

## The Closet

Billy sat in the cold. He had a chill running through him that felt like it started in his spine. It was the kind of cold chill that made your teeth start to chatter. He remembered being so cold with his mom last winter when they went sledding. Before they got cocoa, they both had the chatters.

He asked his mom if people with dentures chatted their teeth, but she said she had all her teeth, so how would she know? I guess she was right. He hoped he would never learn that for himself.

The sun was shining, and where he had curled up and slept was bathed in warmth. He felt the sun start to warm his clothes, and felt the heat start to touch his skin. He looked up into the sky and let the sun warm his face. He felt the sun warm up his eyelids as the bright orange that shined through them forced his pupils closed.

A soft breeze ruffled the trees and the bushes that surrounded him. They sheltered him when the shade had encompassed everything around him. It filled him with a chill that while he slept, it still kept him aware that he was cold. Now at this moment, he finally felt content although a dull throb on both of his lower legs kept his attention.

As he sat there, thinking about his different scrapes and cuts, he heard the hinges of the front door as they announced a visitor. He knew she was going to be coming out. He thought about this morning and when they first arrived here at the house. The sound of the hinges were saying, "Come in, my pretties. You're for supper!"

He heard the front door begin to open wider. Anne was a big woman. It would have to be wide open so she didn't run into it. He giggled to himself, thinking of her walking into the door. He could use one of those voodoo dolls right now. He had seen a show with voodoo dolls in it, and they would be really helpful against mad babysitters. He would take his finger and poke her in the eye like that cyclops that got blinded by a spear. He would spear her eye with his finger.

Among all the ivies and the four-feet-tall bushes as well as the piled leaves and all the overgrown foliage, he was pretty well hidden from view, so he didn't move. He sat as still as he could, and he held his breath. He didn't realize that he was holding his breath until he had to take a sudden gasp for air.

He gasped, and he wasn't sure how loud it was. Every time he ever tried to hide from his mom, he would always have to sneeze. She always found him no matter what he did or how good his places were. His head started to hurt from holding his breath.

He hunkered down and didn't make a sound. He listened for her to come out and say something, but he didn't hear anything at all. It was silent. But her bare feet on the cement porch would render his hearing no help at all. He would let her call out for him until she was blue in the face, and he would stay right here, and when his mom would get here, he would run and jump into her car and tell her to do her best Steve McQueen.

"Get on it, Mom!" He was fixed on his escape when a powerful hand wrapped itself up into his shirt and yanked him upward. He was awed at the strength that this woman had. He felt like he was on a bungee ride, but his armpits got the burn from where she had yanked him up.

She steadied him on his feet until he was standing completely upright in front of her. In one quick movement, she came forward with a fist right into his stomach. Instantly, the pain grabbed him as the air ran out from his lungs from the sudden exit of air.

His legs gave out underneath him, and he began to fall to the ground, but Anne clutched a hold on to the shoulder of his coat and yanked on it, preventing him from hitting the ground. She pulled him up the walkway to the front porch stairs where she then dragged him up the stairs to the front door that was wide open and welcoming him back home.

Anne dragged him into the house and began pulling him along the floor. He did not resist. He did not have any resistance left in him. His feet moved slowly back and forth as she pulled as if he was trying to walk on his own. His jacket sleeves were pulled up to his elbows, forced up by his being dragged along the floor. Slowly, she pulled him along, and it seemed like it was going on forever to him.

It can be a funny thing the way that the mind works, almost as if your subconscious wants to play games with you. When things are going horribly wrong, it seems like it takes forever, like time is standing still or slowed down. At a moment where everything is just oh so fine, the brain speeds it all up, so you can't enjoy the good parts. Does that mean your brain likes the bad stuff that you go through in life more?

Billy was at that point where he was feeling worse than he had ever felt in his whole life. The wounds and pricks and cuts and bruises had all settled into their own little hurt compartments and got comfortable. The dull ache that had focused at one point had now spread so that it was his whole body that had the dull throb. There wasn't a part of his body that wasn't either cold or tired, injured or cramped. He was spent.

She began to pant as if she were starting to tire rapidly as she pulled him through the foyer and down the hall. A groan had begun to replace the panting. He was sure that her dragging him was starting to really wear her down, but he didn't have any fight left in him even if he was able to resist.

She continued to pull him to the end of the hall where going through the door frame, both his shoulder and his leg knocked the doorjamb from her pulling him through the doorway at a strange angle. The pain from hitting the doorjamb didn't even matter. It was like he was immune to the pain. Maybe it was the cold chill that had been running through his blood.

He was exhausted. Although he had slept, the stress of the day had him mentally and physically exhausted. His stomach had cramps from where she had punched him. The pain had eased, but it felt as though he had a bowling ball in his stomach.

She dragged him through the door into her workroom to a heavy wooden door. The room was filled with shelves and tools and boxes with piles awaiting add-ons to their height. The door was rounded on the top and looked like it was made out of long, individual strips of wood glued together to make one strong piece of wood. Its thickness and weight was supported by three hinges that looked as if bats had clung themselves in place to hold the door to its frame. The hinges looked as if they were made out of a heavy iron.

She stopped as they arrived at the heavy wooden door. With one hand tightly gripped on my wrist, she removed a key from around her neck that was attached to a long leather strap. She placed the key in the large eyelet hole and twisted the long key. He heard a heavy click as the door's lock disengaged when she turned the key. She pulled the door open as the hinge screeched from the heavy strain of the door.

She began pulling him forward until his body was lying long ways on the floor. The closet was so big that there was plenty of room to spare.

He lay there motionless as she let go of his wrist and let it drop to the floor. Slowly, the door hinges argued out loud in protest as the door swung closed. Complete darkness enveloped the room as the door slammed shut. The latch engaged, and the lock clicked. It was quiet. It was dark.

# CHAPTER 20

## Route 12

It was sunny all day until they got on to that last leg of their route. They started up Route 12, and this was the part that made her nervous. She did not like being by the traffic as it went whizzing by. To her, it was nerve-racking and extremely dangerous. All it took was one person not paying attention and she would find herself lying in a ditch fifty feet away. That was how far she would fly if somebody hit her going really fast.

Jimmy wanted her to run across the street and do the other side at the same time, but she refused. Instead, she made his ass drive down to the end and then turn around and then come up the other side. It added on about ten minutes, but hell, it was better than leaving a part of her on some jackass's bumper or windshield.

The further they went down Route 12, the worse the weather got. Off to the west, the sky was clear as the sun began to reach for the other side of the world. As they continued up Route 12, that was when the thunder and the lightning kicked up. The weird thing about it was that the storm seemed to be spinning in one spot like a tornado. That was exactly what it looked like.

At first glance, it wasn't noticeable, but she stood still for a moment and noticed the clouds doing a continuous, slow churning in the distance.

"Stupid b——tch, start throwing trash!" she heard Jimmy scream out his window from up in the cab. She looked around the corner of the truck and got his attention so he could see her in the rearview mirror.

She made a cranking motion with her right hand as she lifted up her middle finger with her left. She knew he saw her in the rearview mirror, and she knew that he was one pissed off a———hole up there in the cab of the truck, stewing.

She really shouldn't have done that, but she was getting to the point that she was done with this job. There was no more tomorrows with this job. There was more to life than this. She didn't care. But she was not going to let him get the best of her. It didn't matter what he did; she was going to try to give him what she got. If he was going to piss in her Wheaties, she was going to do the same for him.

Lightning streaked across the sky, and she started getting a bad feeling that she was going to get soaked. Then she noticed that Jimmy had started slowing down. The little a———hole was just hoping that she would get soaked. But the clouds overhead let loose with a thunder and lightning show but with no rain.

She didn't understand it, but it started to get really dark. She kept throwing garbage as fast as she could and was waiting for Jimmy half the time because he had slowed down. The cars started to slow as they drove by. They were probably taking in the show that was up ahead in the sky. She was glad because if someone hit her, she would be dead on this road for sure.

She was looking ahead as she walked alongside the truck and marveled at the show in the sky. About a half mile down the road, she saw a car shoot across oncoming traffic and shoot off the road into a grouping of trees up ahead. At first, she thought that the car would crash because of how fast it was going, but she realized that it must have been a driveway that was up ahead but out of view.

She picked up the speed and finally got Jimmy to try to keep up with her. He probably figured that she wasn't going to get dowsed, so he decided to pick up the pace. She looked up and noticed that the sky was almost black. The lightning bolts in the sky streaked but stayed within the clouds. It seemed like the lightning and the clouds were trapped together in a swirling vortex. The lightning shot across the sky with vigor.

For Audrey, it was now getting completely dark out, and it was almost as if the lightning was the only light there was. The street lights, which were few and far between, did not turn on, or they were out. She started rushing now that Jimmy had picked up the pace.

# CHAPTER 21

## Billy and the Birds

From their perch around him, enclosing him and entrapping him, the walls let in no sound. They isolated him like a wind-wrapped cloud.

The television that wreaked noise rooms away, was silent. The quiet became one with the dark. He lay on the floor, feeling his fear slowly start to creep in. It was the dark that began to consume his fear. It was the darkness that he was beginning to fear most.

The walls were made of wood and plaster, lined on the outside with stone that was supporting the cone-like structure that was directly above him. The cone-like structure's lightning rod on the tip of it, reached toward the angry sky above. As bolts of lightning streaked across the sky, shallow echoes of thunder rumbled.

As he lay there, he looked up, only to see an invisible ceiling. It wasn't a ceiling that he saw, but it was the dark. Were dark and the night the same thing? Were they one and the same? Could you survive in the dark? Would the darkness make you mad?

The questions in his mind drowned out the booming that was coming from overhead. What if there was only dark? And wasn't the dark worse than a monster? A monster you can see. When a monster attacks, you can see it. It has to be there. It is a physical, tangible thing. It can chew you, spit you out even, but it has to see you. If it doesn't see you, then it can't eat you. The dark is different.

The dark can be all around you, and with your eyes closed, it can touch you, and you will never know. Have you ever been touched in the dark? A finger running gently across the nape of your neck?

If you close your eyes and picture that same touch, could it be the darkness that has done the deed? When you open your eyes, you don't see the dark. The darkness sees you. With no sight, you are now the prey, a lioness in the dark. Does it attack or is it the dark that has done the deed? The gazelle can't tell you that now, can it? When it gets dark and the night encompasses everything, then maybe something else will be able to tell you.

Billy had an ache in his back. Sleeping sitting up and the wrong way had made him sore. The floor underneath him was a comfort. It wasn't dirty, for one, and for another, it was way warmer than the ground outside.

First, he went face-first into a basement and then face-first into a pile of leaves that was definitely not a soft landing.

His experience with a pile of leaves was far better than his experience with a nasty dirt floor. But not all that much. That was for sure.

The closet's floor seemed to have a warmth that slowly began to raise his body temperature. It felt as if the floor had begun to heat up. He thought, at first, that maybe the lightning had something to do with it, but he wasn't totally sure. He didn't see how that was possible. It might fry him alive. He knew that from watching shows about lightning. His mom won't let him take a bath either.

He thought it was silly, some of the things that his mom said, but she was probably right. Moms are usually always right. He didn't want to tell his mom that he knew that, but it was true. He really could not think of a single time when she wasn't right, like my tongue on the frozen porch swing. She said my tongue would stick to the chain, and she was right. Then she made me stand there for ten minutes while she threatened to drink my warm glass of water. The ways parents teach us kids are cruel sometimes. It's just too bad that parents don't know that it's cruel.

*I just figured out something that Mom doesn't know*, he thought to himself. His mind was racing with all this. When his mom would get here, he was going to tell her that that was the one thing that he learned today. His mom always said that you learn something new every day. Today he…

"Aaaaawk," said the crow.

Billy stopped in the middle of his thoughts. He heard the subtle voice of a crow. It had a question. The crow had a question, but not of him. He stayed still and listened.

"Aaaaawk," it said again. Its voice was muffled because of the thick ceiling and thicker walls around him. Then there was a reply. A question was asked and answered.

The crow spoke again. Soon a reply came. The two birds in the keeping of their company rang back and forth. Billy listened to their voices. After repeated exchanges, he distinguished their separate voices and could tell them apart. Their conversation came in fits and starts. Moments lapsed and another "aaaawk" rang out and yet another reply. Minutes passed as their calls became more frequent.

Then, suddenly, a third voice appeared. It was different than the two before it. The two speaking before it seemed to be at play, gesturing, saying hello, or maybe they were welcoming each other into the evening. The third wasn't asking a question; the third was the judge. It sat in judgment.

The other two didn't only have a sense, but also an awareness of the order of things. He was the guidepost that led their way. His final say would determine the course of life and death.

*Isn't that what the decision maker is? The decider between life and death? A crow may live or die by the decision of another, a command followed and followed to the death. Are the crows above me also in the dark?* Billy thought to himself. *Does a crow like the dark?* Now the questions began swirling in his mind as the questions of the crows were also repeatedly asked and answered. The third voice was not forgiving. It was a forceful crow call that must have ceased the other two to sit and wait an approval.

Billy heard their wings begin to flap. They were becoming restless. Without warning, a large boom and a crack sounded out in the angry sky above. He could not see, but he could feel the storm overhead.

The crows that were here to accompany him in the dark shifted restlessly and ejaculated calls in their own form of thunderous reply. The crows above him began to speak frantically, although it was muffled. Billy could tell the fear that was injecting itself into them as well.

Billy sat up and got to his feet. Although the ceiling was closer now, he still could see no sign of it. He listened as the crows startled from the loud booms that had begun to increase in dramatic form overhead.

He could not see lightning, but he could sense the clean smell to the air that the lightning leaves behind in its path. His hair in the dark had begun to stand and reach for something that was small and charged.

The dark began to scare him, and the sound was increasing in intensity. He could feel his ears starting to hurt from the cracks of the lightning directly overhead. It was at that point that he could hardly hear the crows doing a dance above him.

The crows above him had completely abandoned the verbal tirades and exchanged them for fluttering wings bent on escape. There was no escape. They had become entombed in a cell of noise. Then the shaking began.

The rumbles of thunder began to shake the house. It was gentle at first like a small earthquake, but as the sounds overhead increased, so did the shaking. It began to get violent. It seemed as if it was up and down, but at times, it felt as if he was shaking back and forth.

As the floor shook harder and harder, he began to struggle to keep his feet. Suddenly, he was blinded by a brilliant explosion of color, and then silence. Suddenly, it was completely silent. The color all around him enclosed him. It encapsulated him.

His eyes hurt at the sudden change from dark to brilliant light. But the discomfort only lasted as long as it took for him to open his eyes. He could see, but yet he could not. He could not see anything that was two feet away from him just moments ago. But what he could see was the vastness before him, and it was infinite.

He could feel himself a part of something different than anything he had experienced before. The feeling of being completely a part of everything overwhelmed his senses, and it became like a thousand joyous moments all wrapped up into a tiny ball and thrown at him like a water balloon. The instant birth of exacerbation filled him as if it was his soul being gifted a place in heaven.

There was a voice, but he could not hear the voice clear enough to make out what it was saying. Maybe it was more like a vibration. He could not distinguish the two, but the vibration seemed to him at that moment to be the more familiar of the two. Did he know another language? Was it a language that he just learned?

He had a feeling in his whole body that answered the question for him. Sometimes, the verbal answer isn't the proper way to reply.

There was no movement around him as he stood there with his arms outstretched; he basked in the silence and the brilliant tones that had overcome his sight. He had never seen such color before.

The color was like the rainbow reimagined with purples becoming something imaginary, almost like the difference between a cartoon and a black-and-white movie, the same but different. *This light was that of the universe*, he thought to himself.

The light was from somewhere else but the light. The light was just that which was moving that was now standing still. It was standing still because of him, because they wanted to see him. Now they were gone. It was but a flash of a moment in time for them. It lasted a minute for him and ten thousandths of a second for them. Yet their time spent together seemed like an eternity.

# CHAPTER 22

## The Storm

A stressful day at work is always just a stressful day at work. But today had been ten times worse than she had prepared herself for. Ever since this morning when she dropped Billy off, she hadn't been feeling very good. For some reason, Billy kept pinging into her head and throughout the day. She had just been getting a sinking feeling.

She had tried really hard to just blot it all out, but it just hadn't been that easy. But the day had been long, and she had had just about enough. All day, she had been thinking about leaving early just to ease her own mind. Billy would probably be more than happy to see her if she was early.

She was starting to get that guilty feeling, but she had to try and put that away. With everything going on, she didn't think that she could handle the littlest blip in the plan today.

Barb had been trying to call, but the combination of her and work was just about at her wit's end with worry. Sometimes, she got so tired of worry. She would like for one day to just be able to wake up and not care. When was the last time she had been able to do that?

She and Billy went up to ride the glass bottom boat on Lake Superior. She was glad it wasn't a cold day because it could get chilly on a boat out on Lake Superior. The weather in Michigan will change in the next hour so, beware. That was the approach that should be taken with those waters. Even she was well aware of that.

They floated over shipwrecks, and she and Billy had a wonderful few days together. Billy absolutely loved going out on the boat on the open water. The two of them went up topside and let the wind run through their hair as the mist from the bow came up over the top of the boat lightly covering them with mist. The two of them turned out to be good travel partners.

Now that Billy was going to have a little brother, she thought that he would settle down a lot. He was really an active kid, and a little brother would be fantastic for him. Tonight she was looking forward to telling him. She and Alex were going to take him out to dinner and share the news together with him.

That was if she ever got her work done. The sickness in her stomach began to bother her again. She had been looking at the clock for the last two hours, but the pile on her desk hadn't moved at all. It was 5:30 p.m., and she was ready to go home, but she wasn't looking forward to the drive out to nowhere.

She punched out and made her way out to the car. The same chill in the air this morning had decided to keep the evening company as well. She pulled her sweater close to her and bunched up as she made her way out to her car. The chill in the air nipped at her.

By the time she got to Route 12, the sunset had begun to bring a glow to the clouds, blocking the sun's view of her. In the distance, she saw violent lightning streaking in a circular pattern of clouds. Ten miles in the distance, it looked like an F5 tornado that was two miles wide. A stroke of fear filled her bones, the marrow becoming like a hot poker under her skin.

The fear made her ache. *Is that storm traveling along Route 12 in the direct path to Billy?* she thought to herself. It was hard to tell, but it looked like a storm. It was getting really dark, and it was all of a sudden as she got closer and closer. Her foot hit the gas, and her car was doing eighty within seconds.

As she looked in the distance straight ahead of her, a lightning storm sat in place. The lightning was intense and continuous. She had seven miles to go. She gripped the wheel tight.

After a ten-minute drive and seeing nothing but lightning lit paths ahead of her, she got closer and closer to the driveway as the lightning streaked across the sky. As she got to the driveway, the lightning and thunder was dramatically reduced. The lightning streaked the sky but was slower and less frequent.

She pulled into the driveway off Route 12, accelerating as she did so. Rocks flew out into the road from the gravel driveway as her tires left the pavement and gripped the stones instead.

The wheels spun when they first hit the rocks. Her foot pushed harder on the accelerator. The trees and the bushes blocked the strong wind that was blowing, but branches littered the path ahead as they fell from the canopy above.

The urgency to see her son grew as the house began to come into view, as her car left the shield of the trees from the lightning streaking across the sky overhead. The lightning lit up the interior of her car and cast an ominous light on the house appearing in front of her.

She pulled up to the front of the house and parked where she had when she dropped Billy off earlier in the morning, the nose of the car displacing bushes as she pulled up close to the house. She tried to keep her composure as she slammed the car's gear shift lever into park and turned the car off. She rushed to get her seatbelt off and tried to open the door at the same time. She was in such a hurry she couldn't figure out where the door handle was. That was how frayed her nerves had become.

She pulled hard on the handle when she found it and half ejected herself out of the car. She pulled on the door to keep herself from falling and slamming it shut all in one motion. She ran around the back of the car but slowed when she made it to the path stones because it was really dark, and she could barely see the ground in front of her.

There was no porch light or any other light for that matter, so it was really dark in the front of the house. She took a glance at the front of the house as she made her way up the stone walkway. In the flash of a lightning bolt, it looked like the roof in the center of the house had collapsed. She walked slowly, but it was with a purpose.

Lightning flared across the sky and lit up the path as she made it up the front walkway steps. The front door seemed to glare menacingly at her at the top of the porch like a huge monster bent on keeping you out of his lair. She made her way up the stairs and was half expecting the front door to be locked, but it wasn't.

She grabbed the handle and slowly pushed the door inward. A squeak from the hinges beckoned her. She stuck her head through the gap. Thunder and lightning boomed overhead and lit up the foyer as she entered. The foyer was disheveled, and the dust that had covered everything turned into chunks of ceiling scattered onto everything.

She stumbled over objects, trying to make her way to the back room where she thought Billy would be. Neatly piled magazines littered the floor along with almost everything else that was once neatly piled. Suddenly, she heard heavy running footsteps coming in her direction out of the side hall. Instantly, she was on guard. As the footsteps got closer to the foyer, her heart began to race.

A large shoulder and body came around the corner, and she looked into its eyes and almost fell over.

# CHAPTER 23

## The Living Room

Anne sat in her recliner and stared straight ahead, slowly rocking back and forth. She had begun to sweat, and the graying hair that was frizzy and in all directions was now starting to cling to her face as the dampness attracted it.

As her head moved back and forth with the movement of the chair, her eyes remained focused on the same spot across the room. There was a television on and blaring voices that were so loud they could chase off three blind mice in a straight line. But she didn't hear it. She didn't know it was there.

The muscles in her feet slowly applied pressure to the floor, pushing the chair slowly back and forth. This was where she was comfortable. This was where she could find peace. That was until the boy started coming around.

She had been able to forget it all. But this boy brought it all flooding and rushing back to her. It had been so many years ago, the memories, memories of the pain. The pain that she had inflicted upon so many. Could she feel guilty? Could she feel remorse? She tried. Oh god, she tried.

Anne's thoughts were rushing through her head so fast that she had started to get confused. She was shaking. Her hands were shaking. The thunder boomed, and it started to get louder as the cracks that rang out from the lightning that was lighting up the room better than the 60-watt bulb ever could.

This little spot in the world was the only place where she had a little bit of peace. But her peace was not like that of most. Her peace was a slice of chaos sliced so thin that the chaos became pointed pain, directed like a spear and inflicted in ways that leave the softhearted cold.

For her, she thought that the peace was shattered. "The peace," she spoke out loud to herself, but as she spoke those words softly, a rumble of thunder made itself known. Panes of glass shook softly with a ripple. It was like when a storm was in the distance. "The storm is here for me!" Anne began to speak, but as she did so, she began to yell, projecting the proclamation skyward.

All her life, she had been waiting for the storm. She had been waiting for the footsteps to come in the night. Mother had always asked her, "What is wrong with you, child?" Her anger. Her mother's anger. The anger that mother had taken out on her. The beatings at night when nobody was home. She was mean, and that was because of the fire. The fire in her guts. The fire in her heart.

"What is wrong, Mommy?" Anne said aloud as her chair continued to rock back and forth. She tilted her head back as the drool that had accumulated in the corner of her mouth dropped down to her chin.

"Oh, Mother, you didn't know?" Anne said, her voice starting to raise and get deeper. She began to take deep breaths, gasping for air.

"What about the footsteps, Mother?" she yelled out. "Did you know about the footsteps, Mother? The footsteps that came to my room at night?" Anne began to rock faster in her chair as her anger began to build. Her anger was building, and the pace of her heart was leaping. Steadily back and forth, she pushed herself as the thunder and lightning overhead began to increase.

"I didn't want anything from any of you!" She picked up a lamp and ejected it from her hand into the screaming television. The glass exploded with a bang that was matched by a thunderous explosion overhead. Sparks and glass flew.

A crack of lightning sounded out. The thunder overhead rattled the windows and the walls. The ceiling overhead began to show signs of strain. The house began to shake back and forth and up and down, and then the shaking erupted.

"The boy!" Anne screamed out. "It's time to make them all pay." Her eyes got big in their sockets. She grabbed the arms of her chair and pulled herself forward to her feet. The shaking made it difficult, at first, to keep her footing, but she put her arms out to her sides to steady herself.

"I have tried to, Mother! I have tried to make them all pay! Every man and every boy!"

The thunder's scream became a roar as lightning filled the room with a continuous flare. The trees outside strained under the pressures of the winds. Large branches lashed across the property outside the window as the house, it seemed, was coming down around her.

She turned and began walking to the back hall that led to the workroom where the closet enclosed the monster. Pictures that neatly guarded their place on the walls were falling all around her. Neatly piled stacks of collectibles fell to the floor and were then thrown about.

When she made it to the back hallway, she was able to put out her arms and hands on the walls as she walked to help her keep her footing. The shuttering and the banging continued. Slowly, she stepped over fallen objects, some of which were now no longer recognizable.

Power lines had broken away from the back of the house with an uproar of sparks. Now the light that was there to guide her way came in fits and spurts. Lightning streaks that had begun to leave the thunder's quiet barely lit her path. The shaking was stopping, and the thunder overhead was becoming a low rumble.

She turned into the workroom where objects were in piles although the darkness hid the piles' ingredients. The door that guarded the boy was as she left it. She approached it as she pulled the key from over her head from around her neck.

As she approached the door, she put the key in and turned the lock. She pulled the door open with a familiar whine of the hinges. Inside, shelves that housed her belongings were empty, and the floor was full of their contents.

There was no boy. She was startled for a moment. She looked again. No boy. She walked into the closet and began kicking around piles of her stuff that was now ruined by the boy! She thought to herself.

Anne heard the whine of the hinges on the door behind her as she flailed about, looking for him. The room became pitch-black as the door behind her shut. She heard a familiar lock go *click*, the click of the lock to the closet.

The darkness was pitch-black. She felt for the door's latch and found it, but it was locked. "Boy!" she screamed out. She stepped back as far as she could until something behind her stopped her progress. She ran at the door as hard as she could and made a heavy impact with it, nearly tearing the hinges from the doorframe.

Her left cheekbone came into contact with the door a moment before her shoulder, and a deep gash opened on her face. In the dark, blood had begun to run down her cheek and began dripping down the front of her.

She stepped back and hit the door again with her whole body. Then the whole door gave way, the hinge side and the latch side at the same time. The whole door fell forward, and she was running over it before it completely fell to the floor.

# CHAPTER 24

## Brandy in the Hall

Brandy waited as the footsteps came closer. When the footsteps got close, what came around the corner stopped Brandy in her tracks. It was Billy. Only it wasn't Billy. His clean gray shirt that he had left the house with this morning was dirty, and it was small and tightly fitted to his torso. His sweatpants that he had on were tightly clung to his legs and came up almost to his knees. It was too small. The little Billy that she had dropped off this morning was now a six-foot-four-inch tall man.

She looked up into the eyes of her son, who now resembled his father right around the time that he went into the military. She always thought that Billy's father was the most handsome man that she had ever met. When he had proposed to her out of the blue and after they had been together for such a short period of time, she couldn't resist telling him yes. This Billy standing before her looked like his father, but it was Billy.

Brandy took a long look into his eyes. He still looked like her little boy, but his features had aged, and he had become a man. She could see that little bit of her in him although the features that he had got from his father were far more prominent.

She was in awe. Then she was in fear. She was staring at a man she knew years ago. Her heart was racing so fast that it felt that it was going to explode out of her chest. She realized that her hands were shaking. The first thing that came to her mind was that there was something wrong with her. *Do I have something wrong with my head that is making my hands shake?* she thought to herself.

"Mom, we have to go!" Billy said to her, but she was so in shock that she couldn't even respond to him. She was in utter confusion. How could it be? Where was my little boy whom I'd already lost so much time with? Did this mean that she would never see him grew up? What about school? How was he going to go to school if he looked like this? How was she going to take him school clothes shopping? Wait, did this mean that she didn't have to go school clothes shopping? The questions raced through her head faster than she could answer them. She was in shock.

"Mom," she heard him screaming to her. His voice sounded like it was coming at her through a tunnel. She was transfixed, looking into his eyes. She was struggling to look away. She opened her mouth to talk, but there wasn't anything coming out. His eyes were the eyes of her eight-year-old boy whom she had cradled as a baby as he fussed in her arms and looked her in the eyes to tell her what was wrong.

She needed a smack across her face to snap her out of the daze she found herself in.

Billy took her shoulders into his hands and shook her to snap her out of it.

"Mom, we have to go!" The urgency in his voice finally snapped her free of the deluge of wonders she found herself ingesting. *So much for giving Billy the news tonight,* she thought to herself.

As that thought raced through her head, Brandy snapped out of a haze and grabbed Billy's large hand into hers and turned and ran toward the front door. Billy's large body was right behind her as she exited the front door.

Lightning shot across the sky, but only the blustered winds followed their race across the sky. The booming thunder had silenced. Darkness greeted them as they exited the front door and raced down the front steps. The nip in the air reached out at them, but neither one noticed. The stones that made a path toward the car looked like little dark holes in the ground.

When he reached the car door, Billy lifted the door handle only to find it to be locked. He lifted the handle again and then a third time, hoping that maybe there was some kind of mistake. He watched his mom as she made her way around the back of the car to get to her door.

When she got to her door, she lifted the handle; the door was locked. She looked at it in a total disbelief. How could it be locked? "No," she said out loud to herself. Her hands went to her sweater pockets, but there was nothing in any of her pockets.

A bolt of lightning streaked across the sky. At the same moment, she looked into the car only to see that the keys were hanging from the ignition; she had never pulled them out.

# CHAPTER 25

## Mom to the Rescue

Billy stood standing still with his arms down at his sides. He was standing outside the closet across the room, looking at the door that, just a few moments ago, kept him on the other side. Now he watched as it sat, guarding only the debris that could have fallen on him. Although the lights were out—and to Anne, it was dark—to him, it was well lit but not by any outside light. It was the night, the darkness, that made everything visible to him. He could see everything crisply and clearly.

"Aaaawk," the judge spoke out.

Billy turned around only to see a two-feet tall crow standing tall on a workbench perched behind him. Billy knew what he wanted. They could see for each other. That was what he wanted to tell him.

"Shh," Billy said to the crow.

The two stood there, listening as Billy began to hear footsteps. They were moving quickly and were coming. He turned toward the door and waited for a figure to appear. Within moments, Anne came around the corner. Billy waited for her to come after him, but she never saw him. It was too dark for her.

She went straight for the closet door. He watched as she took the key off her neck and put it into the lock. She unlocked it and opened the door and stepped into the closet. She began rummaging around. He heard her scream, and then he walked to the door and pushed it shut.

He then felt for the tiny tumbler inside the lock, and when he found it, he pulled on it and engaged the lock. A moment later, Anne began hurling herself against the door. The hinges began to strain after the first impact.

That was when Billy heard his mom's voice in the front hall. He left the light and went back to the darkness. The crow was gone. He began running out of the room and down the darkened hall to where his mother was there to get him.

When he came around the corner and saw his mother, his heart exploded with happiness. However, the look of shock on her face and her small figure instantly registered something different. His mother was stunned while she was looking at him, but Anne was coming, and they had to go.

# CHAPTER 26

## Anne Trips

Billy stood next to the car. He looked over at his mother, only to see that she had a look of dread the width of her face. Her door did not open. He didn't understand why she wasn't getting into the car. He just couldn't wait to get home tonight.

He just wanted to get himself a bowl of cereal and curl up on the couch with his mom and watch some cartoons. He loved it when they fell asleep on the couch together. When she made him go to sleep in his bed at night, that was when he usually got himself into trouble with the monster-thinking.

A scream erupted from behind Billy, and with a quick movement, he turned around, only to see Anne was running out of the front door and down the front steps in his direction, straight at him with eyes blazing red in the middle.

Brandy saw the mad, crazed look on Anne's face as she ran across the front porch and began running down the stairs. She had her eyes fixated on Billy. Her eyes were huge in their sockets. In the nighttime darkness, the whites of her eyes were like the headlights of hell.

Hell was lighting the way for Anne through her deeds, and her deeds were not over yet as far as she was concerned. The boy was the problem. The boy had started all this. The boy had brought all the memories back, and now they won't stop.

They won't stop entering her head and filling her with the thoughts of what she had done. It wasn't wrong what she had done;

she had thought many times. She was the teacher, the teacher of the boys and to make them into real men, to mold them and make them into the form that she saw fit. But none of the boys were fit, not to Anne-Kay Ruth, they were not.

The men that they all became were unfit. That was how Anne saw it, and that was God's word to her. However, the boy had brought all this upon her. The boy was to blame for everything. Anne felt the anger in her explode as she ran down the front stairs.

Blood ran down the side of her face, and her hair clung to the blood that had begun to dry on non-sweat-soaked skin. She had a large pointed object in her hand, which she had raised over her head.

The spikelike object that Brandy saw raised up high in Anne's hand was poised and ready to strike the large chest that now stood out from her son. She could see it in the woman's eyes. Brandy, standing at her car door, whirled around toward the rear of the car.

The gravel that lined the spot where she was parked slid under her feet as she began to run. For an instant second, she feared not being able to run fast enough on the stone to be able to get to Billy before Anne did. She came around the back of the car and started running toward Billy, who was frozen in place.

Anne and Brandy were on a collision course, Anne making her way down the wide cement steps to the front walkway stones, Brandy coming around the back of the car, both intent on making it to Billy who stood watching what was coming at him.

The whole day he had been in fear. That fear was gone. Did he have fear? He couldn't feel any. He watched as everything was seeming to be happening really slowly. The wail coming from Anne ceased to be a wail. He could feel everything as it was happening in slow motion.

He could feel every vibration of the footsteps that Anne made. It sent out a vibration that he could feel. It was as if the nighttime or the darkness acted as if it was like water, sending a vibration or a sound wave. Even the movement of her arms sent out a ripple of vibration. He could feel the vibration, and the vibration was like a picture or a movie.

Anne's wail became more like a flutter. Everything became silent. Then at that moment, when everything became silent, he saw the body of his mother as she threw herself in front of him.

Anne, at the same time, came sprawling forward toward him. He saw her large body as it began to lose its balance and had begun to sprawl forward. The long shaft in her hand stabbed straight out in the direction of the chest of his mother who was now right in front of him.

At the last moment, Anne tripped on one of the stones indented in the ground at her feet and lost her balance. The spike that was gripped tightly in her hand came down in an unnatural stroke and struck Brandy in the chest just above her left breast. The force of Anne crashing into her sent the three of them sprawling in three different directions.

Billy lay on the ground and tried to get his bearings to understand what had happened. He looked over to his mother, only to see her lying on the ground by the back tire of the car.

Anne started to try to get to her feet. Her hands became theaters of pain as she pushed on them, getting her chest off the dirty leaf-covered ground. Her push-up form in the dark rose and began to tower to Billy as she made it to her feet. She had every intention of finishing what she started.

Billy could hear Anne moan in the dark as she struggled to get up off the ground. He could tell that she was injured from the moans that she made as she tried to get off the ground. He could hear her trying to stand, so Billy quickly got to his feet. He looked over at his mother and saw a large spike protruding from her chest.

He looked over and saw that Anne had gotten up onto her feet. Slowly, she turned around, and he saw the wounds on her face, head, and hands from throwing herself against the closet door to free herself. Their eyes locked.

Her eyes were blazed with fury, and then it struck her. The look on Anne's face slowly began to change. It started to become a look of wonder. There was a little boy here; she suddenly realized. Who in god's name was that? She saw the boy's face. She knew exactly who he was. He was big, but he was the same worthless twerp. *I will still kill him*, she thought.

That was when she heard it, and she froze. The clouds began to clear overhead, and the moon began to put a soft glow to the surroundings. Their wings were so large that their sound was like the wind. They arrived on the wind, and immediately it grew quiet. There was no more thunder. There was no more lightning. Clouds gave way, and it was only the swift and quiet motion of the large bodies fluttering in the air that came to a quick standstill among three chosen perches.

Anne saw a large bird land on the car directly behind Billy and one landed to her left and another to her right. Their dark eyes peered at her as though she were the main focus of their arrival. The three crows stared at her and slowly lowered their heads. Their pinpoint vision focused on her, and she could feel the three sets of eyes glaring at her. Their heads were down, but every few seconds, they would raise them as if they were trying to intercept a call to flight. Anne couldn't believe how large they were. Their beaks were six inches long. Their beaks' tip came so sharply to a point that their entry into flesh would be as a hot poker into a balloon.

Because of its height and size, one peck from their beak could be a painful experience. Anne stared in awe at the beasts. Their claws were long, and their sharpened five-inch tips were all pointed in her direction. Anne looked at Billy. She looked at the birds. The crow standing on the roof of the car next to Billy called out "aaaawk!" in a screech that Anne couldn't believe a bird could make.

*The judge has spoken*, Billy thought to himself.

It was the first time in her life that Anne ever felt fear. A pool of urine began to pool at the base of her right foot. In an instant, she turned to run for the front door; but as she did so, all three crows took flight. Billy was right behind them.

Anne turned and began to run up the front porch steps and stopped when the first crow descended onto the top of her head. She felt piercing claws dig into her skull from all directions.

A moment later, something slammed into her chest and clutched her breasts as claws tore through her nipples and deep into her skin.

A large beak slammed into the side of her neck, directly into her artery. Blood began to expel from her body in quantities that would cause her to lose consciousness in a very short time. A third impact hit her hard in the back at almost the same time as the second. It felt as if a bunch of knives had entered her back. She went to her knees as the top of her head came off and all her hair with it.

# CHAPTER 27

## Mom and Billy Chat

Brandy lay on the ground. She opened and closed her eyes a few times. It felt like she had a huge weight on her chest. It felt like she was having a heart attack. *Am I having a heart attack?* she thought to herself. That was the first thing that came to her mind. She went through a symptom list in her head. She could hear in the distance a commotion, but she couldn't see. She was in too much pain to try to turn her head.

She tilted her head forward just a little. The pain from that little movement had her breast feeling like it was on fire. She tilted her head forward and saw the handle of something sticking out of her chest. Then it hit her, and her thoughts began to clear. It was like she had been in a daze.

The handle that was sticking out of her chest she knew was really bad. Breathing was becoming harder and harder. She could feel her head getting lighter and lighter. She could feel her eyelids as she had never felt them before. Her eyelids felt like two weights opening and closing.

She thought of all that she would miss. Was this when my life began to flash across my mind? she asked herself. She started to get cold. A shiver ran up her spine, and then it was "them bugs." It was then that she looked up and saw that the clouds begun slowly parting to reveal a full moon in the starlit sky.

She tried to breathe, but the more she tried to breathe, the more painful it was. She just lay still and tried to hold open her eyes. Very gently, she felt her body begin to lift off the ground. She felt that this was the last moment of her life and that her body had released her soul. She stared into the night.

Slowly, a small shape began to appear before her as she stared up to the sky. A little dot that had begun to grow in size. It was like this little dot was expanding, coming out of the night. The dot slowly began to form the tip of a nose.

Then a nose slowly began to take shape before her eyes. Then the nose became larger, and a face started to come out of the dark. It was Billy's face. Then, very slowly, the rest of his body began to appear. When all of him was completely visible, she was in his lap. His arms were strong. He looked just as beautiful as his father. She became so filled with joy at that moment. She was seeing her son, and the man whom she had loved at the exact same time.

"Anne, where is she?" she garbled the words out in a struggle.

"Shh, Mom, it's all okay." Billy looked into her eyes.

They exchanged a glance of mother-and-son love, and they were both completely fulfilled at that moment. They both knew the outcome. He reached to her face and wiped the tear from the corner of her eye.

"Billy, how?" She looked up to him, but he remained silent and just looked into her eyes.

He cradled her and smiled at her. He wanted her last moments to be happy. It was hard for him, but at this moment, he wouldn't cry. He would be strong for her. He would be a man like the one that now appeared before her.

"Billy?" she said with strain in her throat as it continued to tighten up.

"Yes, Mom?" he said it softly. He wanted her to talk softly so she wasn't strained.

"You're going to be a brother." She tried to smile, but blood began to gather at the corner of her mouth.

"I love you, Mom," he said back to her. He tried to smile, but he couldn't.

"Billy?" she said to him again.

He could barely make out what she was saying now. She was getting weaker.

"Yes, Mom?" He cleared the hair from her face gently using his fingers.

"What happened to you? What are you?" She looked into his eyes. Her last breath was close, and he knew.

"I am…" He waited. He wasn't sure what to say to her at that moment. He, at that moment, had no words to describe what had happened to him. He wasn't sure if he had all the answers himself.

"Aaaawk," a crow blurted out with fervor.

It was the judge, perched and watching as he sat with his mother, keeping watch over them.

"What are you, Billy?" She could barely get the words out as she looked into his eyes in awe of him.

"I am the night," he said to her softly as she took the final inhale of her lifetime.

# CHAPTER 28

## Audrey in the Driveway

Audrey got to the driveway where she thought that car had gone off the road. She stopped. She looked up the driveway, and far up, she could see where the gravel driveway went around a little curve and then disappeared. As the truck sat at the side of the road, she slowly walked up the driveway just a few feet to see if she could see anything.

The sky cleared, and she could hear the truck idling twenty feet behind her. It was then that she heard a scream. She knew a woman's scream when she heard one. This was a woman's scream, and it came with rage. It sounded like a demon had expelled the tones. It was a loud grumbling sound that was mean-sounding and came with a lot of anger.

She started running up the driveway with a little more urgency but looking intently as she went. She looked ahead of her to see her way, but the darkness hid the path of the uneven driveway that would love to send her sprawling.

The length of the driveway was covered with trees, and the light from the starlit sky above did not show her the way. She listened for the gravel stones so that she knew she was still on the path as she made it to the bend in the driveway. That was where the foliage had begun to thin, and the house was in view.

Audrey stopped to look ahead as she made it to the bend of the driveway. The house looked like it oversaw a wonderland of once spring and summer green that had all now faded into something brown and unwelcoming. What she saw next put a chill in her bones and made her stop. She was frozen in place. Her feet would not move. She stared across the opening and saw the car that she had seen shoot into the driveway.

Next to the car, a woman lay on the ground. Well, she wasn't exactly lying there. She saw her body slowly rise off the ground, not her whole body but just from the waist up, as if she were sitting up in an invisible bed just propped up, and then it happened.

A face began to appear, and then the body of a whole man sat there, cradling her in his lap. She stood there mesmerized as he talked to her. Her feet were frozen to the ground, and her heart was beating like she had just thrown a whole truck load of garbage into the back of the truck. For what seemed to her like a very short period of time, he was there, and then he was gone.

The woman was slowly lowered back to the ground. It was then that Audrey's feet began to move and faster than she had ever moved in her life. She ran to the woman's lifeless body and began to check for a pulse.

She rushed through a series of things that she thought would be the right thing to do, but there was no pulse. Audrey thought of all the things that she had seen in her life and all the things that she had had to endure, but this was…

"Aaaawk," says the crow.

Audrey stopped cold and stood still as she stood there, looking down at the woman on the ground in front of her. Slowly, she turned her head and looked behind her, only to see the lifeless body of another woman lying at the base of the stairs that led up to a huge front door. However, it was what else she saw that stopped her heart.

Three crows stared at her, just looking as if they were watching her in a movie and having a snack. One of the two-feet tall birds was standing on the woman's skull. It had what looked to be an eyeball, hanging from a short string clutched in its mouth.

Audrey saw the other two close by, and all three of them just stared at her with curiosity.

"A murder of crows," Audrey heard herself say.

All three birds took flight; one of them appeared to have dropped what was hanging from its mouth when it crested the chimney that still stood tall. She looked down at the body in front of her. She was stunned at what she was seeing. The beautiful woman lying on the ground had a long object protruding from her chest. In the process of trying to help her, she managed to get blood all over her hands and down the front of her clothes.

It became suddenly so silent. *Jimmy? Where is he and where is the truck?* she thought. Anxiety flooded into her veins. It spread like wildfire. What was she going to do? She had blood all over her. If somebody showed up, what would they think? They would think that I did all this. Jimmy would say that I did all this just to get me shitcanned.

Everything she had was in the truck. She started walking toward the road that wound up the driveway. When the road came into view, there was no truck at the end of the driveway. Jimmy left her here, no phone, no nothing, not even a purse. She was pissed.

She was quitting the minute she stepped foot back in that building. She wouldn't have anything else to do with all that crazy shit. She really didn't need it at all. She was done. She put her face in her hands and started crying. "What is going on?" she said to herself.

She heard a footstep. Then she heard another. It was slow and quiet. She froze, but she didn't want to turn around. She suddenly realized that she was more terrified at this moment than ever in her life. If Jimmy was gone and everybody else was dead, who was behind me? Could it be the momentarily silent crows? The crows, she realized, were so tall that if you put all three, one on top of the other, they would be the size of an average man? She heard another footstep. She began to slowly turn around. She just couldn't resist the urge to look. It was dark, but the moon began to put off enough light, and her eyes had accustomed to the little bit of light source.

"You were going to help my mom. Will you help me?" It was a really soft voice that spoke to her.

She turned around completely to see a large man standing in front of her. His shirt was way too small and was tightly strapped to his body. It was frayed and torn, and the seams stood little chance of staying together for much longer.

The sweatpants that he was wearing were so tight that the seams had shredded, and they were barely hanging on to his body. "Oh my god," Audrey said in stunned amazement. "What happened to you?" she said. "I saw you over there," she said and pointed to the woman lying next to the car, "with that woman, and then I saw you. I saw you be there one moment and gone the next. I know what I saw."

"That woman is my mother. She is gone. I lost her. I couldn't save her."

"What do you mean your mother?"

"She is my mother. She dropped me off here so the babysitter could watch me this morning."

"Babysitter?" Audrey said, but she was getting more confused by the moment.

"Yes, my mom brought me here this morning. That woman locked me in the closet."

Audrey put a hand out to him and touched his shoulder. "Wait, you mean the woman over by the steps?"

"Yes, she stabbed my mother."

Audrey was stunned to a silence. She didn't even know where to begin. "You look like a twenty-year-old man? How old are you?"

Billy looked at her, and he stepped a little bit closer to her. "I'm only eight."

"You mean to tell me that that woman dropped you off, and now you look like this?"

"Yes, something happened to me and the birds while we were in the house."

"What do you mean birds? The birds were in the house with you?" Audrey asked him in puzzlement.

"Yes, they were above me. Now I can see them above me now."

"You mean to tell me that you can see them up in the sky? The pitch-black sky?" Audrey said without an ounce of belief.

"Yes, I can see them, and I can feel them. I can see what they see, and they can see what I see. I look out for them, and they look out for me. They protect me. That is what they have to do. For that, they may roam for as long as they wish to have wind beneath their wings to take them. Then they can go to the lights to be with the brilliance that awaits them when they wish."

"Brilliance?" Audrey asked with the questioning tone that said "Yes, I do want an answer."

"Yes, the brilliance. That is where my mother is. That woman over there? That was my mother, but that is just a shell now. The real her is perhaps anywhere. I know she is happy, but I won't see her anytime soon, but I will."

"You mean see your mother? Like how?"

"You wouldn't understand. You couldn't understand if I tried to tell you," he said this in an explanatory way, but he began to get quieter as he spoke. "Your kind are not like their kind," he said to her, not realizing that he had excluded himself.

"Wait a minute, what do you mean my kind and their kind. What kind does that make you if you're not my kind? Billy, what are you if you're not like me?"

"What am I?" He looked at her in the eyes, not certain entirely of what to say to her. "What am I?" he said again, and he looked down. His despair seemed to come at him all at once, and she noticed it. She felt for him. She knew he was devastated.

"I am the night. When it is dark, it becomes a part of me. When it is dark, I become a part of it. If I want to be there, I go there. If I want to be here, like I am now with you, then I will be with you. It is two worlds, this world that you can see and the other world that you can't. In that world, there is no time in the dark. When I am one with the dark, there is no time. When my mother died and I left her there on the ground, I went to see my grandmother. I watched my grandfather die. He knew I was there, and he let go. Then I walked for hours and went down to Traverse Bay and skipped stones for a while. When I came out of the dark back here, you were getting up from my mother's side. I followed you to the end of the driveway. I was so afraid that you were going to run away. I need your help. I'm eight, and I don't know what to do."

He looked at her, and the two remained silent.

"We have to get to my apartment," Audrey said to him with urgency in her voice.

"Wait!" Billy said to her. He turned around and ran off into the dark toward the house. A minute later, he came back with a blanket clutched in his arms.

Audrey grabbed Billy by his arm with a gentle touch, and the two of them made their way off into the night.

# CHAPTER 30

## A Long Walk

Audrey was really struggling from the long two-hour walk that she had to endure. She did a lot of walking, but nothing had prepared her for the walk that she had to take tonight. She had slung garbage for ten hours, and then the events of the evening had her exhausted. She felt like she had a purpose for once though.

The two of them had spent two hours talking on the walk back here to her apartment. The two of them had decided that neither of them wanted to stay here. Neither of them had anything here for them. Billy had lost his mother and his grandfather. It was all so much more than he could take. Audrey was there for him. The two of them had vowed a pact to each other, and there were three more souls in agreement high above, looking down over the two of them.

When she had asked on the walk back here what had happened to him, she walked in amazement as he spoke to her.

"They made me one with my greatest fear," he began. "They did it out of fear for me. What I was was something that when they—I'm not sure how to say it, but…when they crossed my path, they sensed an unnatural fear. Something that they couldn't understand.

"To them, the fear was like a dog's strong sense of smell for a human body when it's taught to look. What was my greatest fear at the time? Monsters. But at that moment in time when they crossed my path, it was the dark.

"They knew that as they were passing by. They travel using the dark. They ride it like a train. Life in the universe? You have no idea what's out there when you look up at night, the stars on a clear night that explode when there is no light to fight it.

"Worlds beyond worlds that are endless in time. You know, they travel so fast that making it through our galaxy takes only as long as it will take you to put a period on the end of this sentence.

"I look like this because they stopped for a fraction of a second to see me, to be in awe of me. They have never seen anything like you or me before. But everything before them as they travel becomes like a shock wave.

"That's how the house got destroyed. It was like a shock wave, and being a thing of the dark, they made me one with the dark. In the dark, my body charges. It is like when you sleep. At night, I feel refreshed like I just slept all night. But I think of the day. What will the day do to me?" he had asked her.

"What about the birds? What happened to them?" Audrey had to ask him.

"I'm not sure what happened to them. They had a fear, but I'm not sure what it was. I may never know. Maybe they will find a way to tell me," Billy said.

"I'm not really sure? You mean you don't know?" Audrey replied back.

"How could I know? I'm only eight. I don't know anything. Do you know why I look like this? Because for just the fraction of a second, they stopped in their travels to see my such strong fear of the dark, and they couldn't understand.

"It was a pinpoint in time, an accident really. I spoke to them, but that's not really the right word to use. I saw the light, and everything was beautiful, almost too much to handle. It's funny because they are in the dark when they travel, and when they are not traveling, they become a brilliant light. That's what you see far off in the universe. You see them sitting still."

She was startled and amazed. She really had no idea what to ask him. She thought, *How do you ask a fundamental question after hearing a story like that?* She wasn't sure who or what she was walking to her apartment with. Should she be terrified? An eight-year-old boy? She had so many questions that she didn't know where to start.

But she did know that he was a boy. She could hear it in his voice and feel it in his mannerisms as he spoke. She had pity for him. He was dirty from head to toe, and he looked sad. But what he said to her left her no doubt of exactly who she was traveling with.

"When we get to your house, can I have a bowl of cereal?"

Audrey stopped dead in her tracks and stared at him. It was then that she saw the man and the muscles and the beautiful face that was looking back at her. She was momentarily transfixed by him. "Yes, I can get you a bowl of cereal," she said back to him with a smile on her face.

Audrey put her key in the lock and jiggled the door to get the door-knob to work and pushed the door open slowly as if she was expecting somebody to be there. It was quiet. She entered the door, and Billy entered in after her. She went around the corner and flicked on the light, bringing the whole room into view. Billy's eyes hurt for a moment with the sudden rush of light. Audrey went into the kitchen and went straight for the fridge to make sure that she had milk.

Billy followed her into the kitchen and sat down at the kitchen table and just stared down into his lap. His hands were so big. He looked down at his crotch, and he was so much bigger down there than he was this morning. He peed on a tree as they were making their way here, and when he pulled himself out, he almost fell on the ground. He was so much different in so many ways that he just felt overwhelmed. *What is going to happen to me?* he thought to himself.

Audrey set a bowl down in front of him with a spoon. He looked up at her and thanked her. "Can I have the prize at the bottom?" he asked her seriously.

"Billy, there are no more prizes in the bottom of a cereal box. They quit putting prizes at the bottom of the boxes because too many children were getting killed by their parents for digging down into the damn bottom of the boxes."

He started laughing, and then so did she. They laughed and laughed.

*****

Billy disappeared into the bathroom to put on the clothes that belonged to her father who was also a pretty big man. For some reason, her mother insisted that she keep some of the boxes of his clothes as a memento. Audrey really didn't understand how that could be a memento, but she kept them anyway.

It was then that she heard the front doorknob turn. She sat completely still as she listened closely. She heard the bath water start in the bathroom, but she was listening toward the front door. Then she heard it again. The front doorknob jiggled again, and then she knew.

She heard the door slowly slide open. She froze. She slowly turned toward the bathroom door to see if it was all the way closed. *He will not hear in the bathroom*, she thought to herself.

She was sitting on the bed next to her nightstand, and she looked toward the front door hallway, and there he was, standing there with a gun pointed right at her chest. She couldn't move. She never, in a million years, would have thought that he would actually have come to her house, but here he was, the legendary asshole, Jimmy.

"You stupid bitch, did you think that I would take that shit from you? You know what? I don't just want to have sex with your stupid ass. You want to know what I'm going to do? Because you are everything that I hate about a b———tch."

She sat there in silence as he spoke.

His finger was on the trigger, and she knew that if she so much as moved that he would just pull the trigger. She knew he was here for business. She just had a gut feeling that he wasn't going to be letting her just walk out the door. He was getting what he wanted one way or the other. She glanced at the bathroom door. Then Jimmy's eyes followed hers. He looked back at her.

"You know what I'm going to do to you?" he said and waited for her to say something. "Did you not understand what I'm saying to you?"

Audrey couldn't think about anything but the bathroom door staying shut.

"I'm just going to shoot you right here, right now," Jimmy said with an utter hate in the base of his throat.

Her hate for this asshole had begun to build. She was ready to jump in his direction when the bathroom door opened, and Billy walked out of it with only his supertight black sweatpants on. His chest stared out at the two of them as they both turned to look in his direction at the exact same time.

Jimmy saw Billy, and Billy stopped cold in his tracks. He stared at Jimmy and looked down and saw the gun that was now pointed directly at him.

"What the hell is this?" Jimmy said, looking at Audrey.

"Leave him alone. He is only a kid. Just leave him alone." After Audrey said that, she thought just how ridiculous that sounded as Jimmy stared at a perfectly fit, large man staring back at him. Jimmy laughed.

A large boom rang out as Jimmy pulled the trigger of the gun that was pointed right at Billy's large chest. The window that was behind Billy when Jimmy pulled the trigger exploded almost as loud as the guns report.

Billy went backward through the window, spraying glass in all directions. He had hit the window so fast that glass shrapnel landed at Audrey's feet all the way across the room. Audrey, now on her feet, stared at the window in horror. She turned to Jimmy, and just as she started to charge at him, a huge bird came flying in through the window.

It went directly for Jimmy's face. Its talons were at Jimmy's skull in the flash of a second. Part of Jimmy's scalp was stripped off when the bird flew at him, and then another large bird hit him in the chest. A third entered the room and came straight at him. The first bird then came and landed on the nightstand next to Audrey. Jimmy's hands went to his skull, only to realize that it was hairless.

Just as the first bird retreated, two other birds came through the window and made impact with him before he could so much as turn around. Jimmy saw them and dropped the gun to the floor. He turned and grabbed the front door and fought his way out the door as the two crows clawed and clutched at him, slicing open his skin and his shirt. He hit at them and forced the door closed behind him, trapping the birds inside with Audrey.

Jimmy ran down the hall and made his way down the stairs to the building entrance. As he ran out the front door of the building, something slammed into the back of him. He ran, and he ran as fast as his legs would take him. He went around the corner of the building, and he knew there was a police station right across the field. As he ran, something else hit him and almost knocked him off his feet. He looked behind him as he ran and saw two large black birds twenty feet above him.

*****

Audrey ran to the window where broken glass covered everything and looked out to the cement street below. There was no Billy lying on the pavement below. "Where did he go?" Audrey said out loud.

"Right here," Billy responded in his little boy voice.

Audrey turned around to see Billy standing there, all 230 pounds of him standing tall. She was a tall woman, but she would have to look up into his eyes.

"I thought he shot you!" She sounded so worried. She looked at his chest to see if he had been shot. She didn't see a wound, but she couldn't look away from him either. *He is a beautiful man*, she thought. She wanted to run to him, but her feet were frozen to the floor. *He is a boy*, she had to remind herself. She had to be the strong one.

"I jumped out the window. He didn't shoot me," Billy said to her in a humorous way.

"You jumped?" she said with utter fear in her voice.

"Yeah. Them birds were coming in the window after him, so I got out of their way."

"Jimmy! Where's Jimmy?" she said with desperation in her voice.

"You don't have to worry about him. He's being judged as we speak."

*****

Audrey's legs gave out, and she fell to the bed. She sat there as the two-feet tall crow perched on her nightstand and stared at her. She was in awe of its poise. It stood tall, and it waited. She was too tired to move. This was the moment where the heroin collapses from exhaustion. Billy looked at the crow as it stood tall. The crow looked back at him.

"Aaaawk," the crow sounded off, and it left its perch on the nightstand and was gone out the window.

Audrey stood up from the bed and went over and hugged him. They embraced, and neither one of them let go.

The End

# EPILOGUE

"We start off tonight's broadcast with the news of a gruesome murder. The body of a thirty-six-year-old woman and the body of a sixty-five-year-old woman were discovered by the garbage man at a home off Route 12. Apparently, one of the bodies was so mutilated that the body couldn't be identified, but they do believe that it is the body of the homeowner.

"In related news, police are looking for an eight-year-old boy, believed to be the other victim's son. The police are working on details related to his possible disappearance."

Mort Crim, the broadcaster, shook his head before reading the next story. Then he slowly began as though he couldn't believe it.

"In other news, we have a strange story coming to us just in the last few minutes, so we are still working on the details. The body of a man was found not far from an east side police station. Police believe that a man was trying to make his way through Wichita Park last night to get to the police station.

"His body was found about a hundred yards from the back of the building. What police discovered were pieces of his remains as far as a half mile away. Police believe that pieces of the man's remains were removed as he ran to try and make his way across the park to the police station."

"Wow, that sounds like he paid the price of a piece of flesh with every step he took," one of the other broadcasters said in reply.

"We now switch to the weather." Mort pointed to Johnny who was standing in front of a green board, waiting for his que to do the weather.

"Looks like rain, Mort," the weatherman said with a grim tone in his voice.

"Well, if they don't find all the pieces of that man now, they might have a hard time finding them at all," the other man behind the news desk added.

"After today's rain, I guess they never will," he replied.

"Either that or the crows will find them," Mort interjected.

"Yes, they will, Mort. Yes, they will."